A DOG WITH TWO TALES

ELLEN RIGGS

BOUGHT-THE-FARM
MYSTERIES

A Dog with Two Tales

Copyright © 2020 Ellen Riggs

ISBN 978-1-990613-77-7 D2D Paperback
ISBN. 978-1-990613-10-4. AudioBook
ASIN B085BQT5LH Kindle
ASIN 1989303463 Paperback
ASIN. B0C4G59G98 AudioBook

Publisher: Ellen Riggs
www.ellenriggs.com
Cover designer: Lou Harper
Editor: Serena Clarke
2501191223

CHAPTER ONE

I was running full-tilt down an alley behind a derelict warehouse when my phone rang. Why hadn't I ditched it before I fled? Ignoring a call was hard for me. It felt unprofessional. That said, I'd just left an executive meeting without a word of explanation, which was the epitome of unprofessionalism. No wonder people were calling. They probably thought I was desperately ill, not sprinting away from the office like an athlete. A clumsy athlete, mind you. One who clearly spent her days in a suit behind a desk. But I was making good time, all things considered.

Fumbling in my pocket for the phone, I managed to check the number and then punch the right button, all without slowing down. "Hey Jilly," I said, puffing hard.

"Where are you?" she said. "And what the heck are you doing? Did you take up CrossFit without telling me?"

"Just out for a little jog." I slowed slightly so I could hear her better. "What's up?"

"Keri Browning said you left an important meeting and then vanished without a trace. She thought it must be personal so she reached out to me."

I finally dropped to a fast walk. "So I can't even have a panic attack without it becoming a federal emergency?"

There was a pause at the other end. "A panic attack? Nothing flusters you, Ivy Galloway. It's your superpower."

"Not anymore, apparently." I looked around, struck by the dinginess of the neighborhood. Eight years ago, I'd bought a condo nearby to be close to corporate headquarters. I'd expected the neighborhood to transition, but it hadn't changed much. I never took the back route because it didn't feel safe.

"Tell me what happened." Jilly's tone was soothing, as if talking someone off a ledge. I suppose that's exactly what she *was* doing.

"Wilf announced a major global downsizing," I said.

"Okay, well that's bad news, but you'll never be downsized. How often has Wilf said you'd be the last one standing if the company folded? You'd still be packaging people out. That's the upside of being in human resources."

"I'm not afraid of losing my job, Jilly," I said, as my legs started pumping again. "I'm afraid of *doing* my job."

She paused to take that in. "Right. Someone's got to do the actual downsizing and I guess that's you."

"Who else but the grim reaper?" I asked. "Three years ago I crisscrossed the country firing people and destroying their lives. Now I have to do it again on a global scale."

"That nickname is *so* inappropriate. You should have lodged a complaint against Wilf."

"With whom? I'm the senior HR manager."

"Ivy, can you just stand still for a minute and listen to me?"

"If I stop moving, I'll die. That's how it is with sharks like me. Wilf said so. He meant it as a compliment."

"*Stop. Right now.*"

She'd never used that tone with me before. Jilly Blackwood was a diplomat, all smooth edges and a voice like honey.

"Stopping," I said.

"You're not. I can still hear your footsteps."

"You wouldn't stop either if you were where I am," I said, but I stopped anyway.

"We'll get to that in a minute. First I want to ask you a different question." She waited until my breath evened out and then said, "What do I do for a living, Ivy?"

"You're a headhunter. Best in all of Boston."

"Which means I can get you out of the Flordale Corporation instantly if that's what you want. You don't need to spend the next year firing people." There was a rustle at her end and I could tell she was getting her things together. "Why didn't you tell me you were miserable before?"

"The water got hot so gradually I only realized today I was about to boil to death."

"No one's dying. Just relax. And now you can tell me where you are, because I'm coming to meet you."

"I'm in an alley about a mile from the office. Hyperventilating."

"Look around and tell me what you see."

I recognized the strategy for calming panic attacks, and although the worst was starting to subside, I played along. "I see a row of tall sunflowers against a garage."

"Sunflowers?" Now I could hear the click of her shoes on the tile in her office hallway. "That's unusual for an alley."

"They're in someone's backyard. It's kind of grubby and stinks to high heaven. There's a lot of dirt with some patches of grass and— *Oh!* There's a black and white dog."

"With the sunflowers?"

"Yeah. Poor thing is chained to a tree. Looks like a sad little heap in the grass." I leaned over the chain-link fence. "Hey puppers. How ya doing?"

The dog lifted his head and his long muzzle and pointy ears swivelled toward me.

"What breed is he?" There were street noises at Jilly's end now. She was ready for takeoff.

"Border collie. He has one blue eye and one brown. I can see that from here, but he won't come over. He seems... depressed."

I reached into the yard and offered my hand. The pup finally stood up and I gasped. "Oh Jilly, he's so skinny. And there are bare patches in his fur. This dog's been neglected."

"Ivy, don't do anything crazy, okay?"

"When do I ever do anything crazy? I'm the opposite of crazy."

"I know you are."

I took a deep breath and let it out. Jilly was my best friend—my only friend, actually—and we'd known each other since college. When I'd joined Flordale, she said it was like I'd taken vows of propriety. It was true that as an HR rep, I always felt pressured to set a great example. Most of the time I avoided the limelight and kept my lips sealed. I was always sensible.

Until today. Today I'd cracked. And once that started, it was hard to stop.

The dog came toward me, dragging a long, heavy chain. He looked young, less than a year old, and had never filled out. Tears filled my eyes as I saw patches of bare skin covered in scratches. The white areas of fur were grimy.

"Jilly, promise me you won't try to talk me out of helping this dog," I said. "I'm not leaving him to suffer."

"I promise. Just tell me where you are. The cab's getting close now."

Jilly could always get a cab, anytime, anywhere. It was one of *her* superpowers, along with the ability to charm everyone, male or female, old and young.

I gave her the directions and sank to the ground outside the yard. The earth was damp from all the rain we'd had recently. "Just think... If you hadn't ordered me to stop right here I never would have seen him. This is like a mission from dog."

She laughed as the door slammed. "We do missions now?"

"It's against type for a grim reaper, I'll admit." I stuck my fingers through the fence and the pup inspected them. "But that's not who I am anymore. Starting today."

"What exactly do you want to do, starting today?"

"I want to rescue this dog, and then maybe move home."

"Home! To Clover Grove?" There was an edge of panic in Jilly's voice for the first time. "Ivy, what's really going on? You said nothing could take you back to that hick town."

"That may have been hyperbole." I crossed my legs and settled in. "And this is a weak moment. A weak day. Daisy called this morning."

"Ah. Things are making more sense now. Your sister laid a guilt trip on you?"

"Not Daisy, but I could feel Mom pulling the strings behind her. I haven't been home in years."

"And now you're facing the prospect of global travel so home has more appeal."

The pup finally touched my fingertips with his cold, wet nose. I felt a little shock, followed by an odd sense of calm. There was something special about this dog. I just knew it.

"I don't believe in Flordale anymore," I said.

When I was recruited out of college 10 years ago, Flordale had been a small specialty food company. The mom and pop operation had long since disappeared in mergers and acquisitions, and with each stage of growth some of the "human" in human resources slipped away. Jilly had tried to lure me into her company many times, but a misplaced sense of loyalty trapped me there. I kept hoping things would change.

"I agree it's time to go, but you need a solid exit strategy," she said. "At your level, it's all about reliability and integrity. You don't want to look—"

"Erratic? Crazy?"

"You know about the importance of reputation. Of appearances."

I pressed my face against the wire and the pup licked my nose.

"Wilf wouldn't hesitate to sabotage me despite all I've given to the company."

"How about we find you a rebound job, just until the real thing comes along? We'll build in some time for you to visit Clover Grove before you start. What do you think?"

"First I rescue the dog and then I beat it out of Boston. You coming?"

"To Clover Grove? Never. What's a headhunter going to do in hick town?"

"Start a café. We both know your secret passion is cooking and the last time I was there it was hard to get a decent meal."

"Don't tempt me," she said. "And what's *your* secret passion?"

"I'm looking at him now. This dog has the most intelligent eyes I've ever seen."

I dug around in my purse and found some beef jerky and crackers I kept on hand for the many nights I worked late. As I offered small bits to the starving dog, he stood on his hind legs and did a perfect pirouette of little hops. Then he solemnly offered a paw, which I poked my fingers through to accept. His honey-brown eye seemed to pour warmth into my cold heart, while his blue eye looked deep into my soul, or what was left of it.

"What's going on?" Jilly asked. "You're awfully quiet."

"I've never known a dog like this and I grew up around lots of them. I've always wanted a pup but I guess I was waiting for the right one to come along."

"One that belongs to someone else."

"He doesn't belong here. He's neglected. Dirty. Scrawny. And yet he was obviously loved at one time. By his breeder, I bet."

"What's that noise?" she asked.

"He's talking to me. He makes these odd mumbling sounds."

"Don't tell me you understand him."

"Not yet. For the moment all I know is that he's grateful and he wants me to take care of him."

There was a long, low sigh at the other end. "Oh, Ivy. Don't get too attached, okay?"

Her words triggered a cascade of sorrow in my heart. "That's what my mom used to say before she confiscated a pet. With six kids, we could never afford extra mouths to feed. The animals only stayed long enough for us to fall in love and then she got rid of them."

"Let's not talk about your mom, right now," Jilly said. "Anyway, I'm going to hang up and call you back in a minute, okay?"

"Sure." I pressed end and reached into my bag for a bottle of water. Pouring a little into my cupped fingers, I let the dog drink.

"You know what, little buddy? We were destined to meet today and change each other's lives."

He offered another mumbled monologue that sounded like agreement.

"You're a regular poet. I can tell you're asking me to bust you out of here, and I'm going to find a way." The pup whined and I continued, "It looks bleak, but keep the faith. They don't call me the grim reaper because I give up easily."

We both looked up at the sound of steady clicks on pavement. Jilly was coming toward me looking as out of place as the sunflowers in the alley. She was a petite, natural beauty with blonde hair and a smile as warm as this early summer day.

"Ivy, get up," she said, offering her hand. "Your suit is covered in mud."

"I'll throw it out with all the rest of my suits. I don't need them anymore."

The pup had curled up against the fence, letting me scratch his ears. Every so often he turned to lick my fingers.

"How about we go and buy this little guy some kibble, while we make a plan?"

"I've got a plan. I'm climbing this fence and taking him. End of story."

A door slammed and we both jumped. An old red car had pulled into the driveway and a man was standing at the gate to the yard. He wasn't tall or muscular, but he had two sleeves of tattoos and a frown that sent out shock waves.

"Yo, blondie!" he yelled. "Get away from my dog."

The pup pushed his head into my palm, trembling. Meanwhile, Jilly pulled on my shoulder to get me to stand. "We'd better go," she said. "He looks mean."

"Don't make me come over there," the guy shouted. "I protect what's mine."

"Liar," I muttered, scrambling to my feet and resisting as Jilly towed me down the alley. "We can't just—"

"Discretion is the better part of valour," she said. "Time for a new plan, my friend."

CHAPTER TWO

The next day was Saturday, so I didn't need to deal with the fallout of my abrupt departure from Flordale's executive boardroom. Instead I met Jilly in the alley in the afternoon armed with kibble, water, bowls and everything the pup might need if we failed to liberate him. I'd even stopped at a veterinarian and tried—unsuccessfully—to talk them into giving me flea and worm medication. They wouldn't be getting my business once I had the pup in my care.

After checking to make sure the red car was gone, I dropped the bowls over the fence and poured kibble in one bowl and water in the other. A long string of saliva dripped from the dog's muzzle but he sat politely till I said, "Okay."

"Impressive," Jilly said, watching him gulp the food. "You're quite a gentleman, Tux."

"Keats," I said. "His name is Keats."

"Keats? Like the poet?"

"Exactly. This guy knows how to recite. Wait till you hear his sad tale."

"In the meantime, you can tell me *your* sad tale." She'd dressed down today in jeans, a powder blue cashmere cardigan and tan suede boots. Jilly didn't really go more casual than that. You never knew when you might bump into a client or meet a new prospect.

I'd worn black jeans and a lightweight black jacket to hide the dirt. Already my knees were damp and muddy from kneeling beside Keats to give him a scratch.

"Animal Services basically sucks," I said. "I called yesterday and they said they sent someone around this morning to check on Keats." I pointed across the yard to the two rusty bowls tipped upside down. "Apparently if a dog has food, water and shelter, they can't do anything about it."

"Shelter? What shelter?" Jilly sounded horrified. "Surely they don't mean that upended box? If he ever fit into that, it was months ago."

"And the bowls are empty, just like they were yesterday. The owner had time to yell at us but not to feed and water the dog."

She stared down at me with sharp green eyes. Her glossy lips pressed together for a moment. Then she said, "So what are we going to do about this situation?"

My heart filled with relief. I was determined to help Keats, but knowing Jilly was on my side gave me courage.

Pulling a leash and collar out of my pocket, I said, "I was thinking I could just, you know, take him."

"That man looked dangerous, Ivy. If he came after you, it might not end well."

"What's he going to do to me?"

"Follow you to your condo? Call Animal Services or the police?" She shrugged. "The options are many and none of them good for you." I started to protest and she held up a manicured hand. "Or the dog, Ivy. Think of the dog."

I was still so outraged that I couldn't trust my own judgment. No doubt some of that stemmed from what had happened at work, so I had to trust Jilly to guide me to make the right decisions. "Okay. No daring dog thefts. What do you suggest?"

She gave me a brilliant smile. "We use your HR skills. When Prince Charming gets home, let's go around front and talk him into believing that giving you the dog is the very best thing he could do right now. If you can convince people that getting fired is the life change they truly need, you can convince this loser that caring for another living creature is too much of a hassle."

"Right," I said. "He keeps the dog chained up back here so he obviously has no great love for him. I will help the guy out by taking Keats off his hands."

There was a roar of a faulty muffler and we moved out of sight as the red car pulled in. After waiting a few minutes, we nodded at each other and went back.

"Can I make a small suggestion, Ivy?"

I was already walking down the narrow lane beside the yard, with Keats following on the inside dragging the heavy chain. "Yeah?"

"Don't call the dog Keats in front of this guy. I sense he's not the type to appreciate poetry."

I gave her a look over my shoulder. "I may be having a crisis of executive confidence but I can handle a lowlife animal abuser, Jilly."

She raised groomed eyebrows that were a shade darker than her highlighted hair. "Normally you're the soul of tact, but you're still on edge, my friend. Just dial things back till you get the dog on your leash. And don't actually *show* him the leash, either."

"Are you going to stage direct my every move?"

Heels clicking on the cracked pavement, she laughed. "I'm sure going to try. I want you to have this dog, Ivy. I can tell you have a connection already."

Keats reached the end of his chain and let out a heartrending wail.

Turning, I held a finger to my lips. "Quiet. Listen to Jilly, Keats. We need to play our cards right."

He sat and wrapped his long skinny tail around his paws. There was a tuft of white hair on the end of his tail. One day that would be a glorious plume rising over long grass as he ran through a meadow. I could see it clearly in my mind. We were going to—

"Ivy? You okay?" Jilly said, as I stood staring at the dog.

I shook my head to dispel the vision. "Maybe you should do the talking. Like you said, I'm not quite myself right now."

She nodded. "I'll turn up the charm. It won't be the first time I've had to cater to fools."

We fell silent as we took the stairs together. Jilly smoothed her hair and applied fresh lipstick. Looking good was half the battle in her line of work, she said. The other half was a combination of presence, brains and integrity. She had all that in spades.

Meanwhile, I plucked an envelope out of the mailbox, examined it and put it back. Now I knew his name. I also knew that he didn't look after his house any more than his dog. There was a rusted-out fridge sitting beside the porch and the eavestrough was dangling dangerously.

Jilly pressed the doorbell and stepped back to stand beside me, smile in place.

The inner door opened and a scrawny man with mousy, thinning hair stared at Jilly through the dirty glass of the screen door. His small brown eyes lit up for a second but then he scowled.

"Weren't you the one trespassing yesterday?" He opened the screen door for a closer look. "You selling something?"

"I guess you could say that." Jilly's smile stretched almost to the point where the ends met behind her head. "You see, we fell in love with your dog yesterday. He's absolutely adorable. But it seemed like he might be bored. Border collies are so high energy."

He spun his index finger in circles. "Get to the point, lady. I don't have all day."

"I can tell you're a busy man." Her voice was still as sweet as cotton candy. "How could you have time for a dog—one that's barely more than a puppy?"

"And...?"

"I'd love to take him off your hands. I'm looking for an active dog I can take on trail walks."

He looked her up and down. "I don't buy it, blondie. Those boots only walk in malls."

"What I'm trying to say is—"

"Save your breath." He started to close the door. "That dog isn't going anywhere. I need him."

"Please." Jilly's voice went up a notch. "He'd be so well loved. Won't you reconsider?"

"No, no and... no." He gave a little laugh. "Bug off."

I had no choice now but to jump in. I did it literally by sticking my boot in the crack of the door just as he started to close it. "How much?" I said, getting straight to the point.

He looked startled, as if he hadn't really noticed me before. That happened a lot, particularly if Jilly was there to draw all eyes.

"Get your foot out of my door." Then he added, "What did you say?"

"I said, how much for the dog?" My voice was calm and I adjusted my expression to HR neutrality. "Name your price."

"The dog isn't for sale. Like I said, I need him."

"I understand you're very attached," I said. "But he's hardly a guard dog."

"He does what I need, aside from attracting do-gooders like you. He's a dog. Period." He looked me up and down, from my sensible, low maintenance shoulder length hair, to my even more sensible boots. "You're the type to swaddle a dog up and rock it like a baby. I can tell."

"Actually, I'd love to teach this dog how to herd sheep. That's what he was bred for. His calling."

"The only calling I hear is the toilet. It's time for my constitutional. So if you—"

"Mr. Roxton," I said. "I really want to buy your dog. I'm sure I can match whatever you paid for him and more."

His eyes were mere slits. "How do you know my name?"

I shrugged. "May I call you Ron?"

"No. You can call out goodbye as you're leaving my property."

"Ron, I find it hard to believe you'd turn down good money for this dog. You have a nice house. You must be a smart businessman."

He rolled his eyes but curiosity won out. "What's so special about this dog? He's just like any other stupid mutt. Couldn't teach him a single trick."

My lips pressed together to quell the hot anger bubbling up.

Jilly touched my arm. "If that's how you feel about him, you surely wouldn't miss him."

"I'll pay you well," I said. "How about a grand?"

His thin lips worked for a second as he thought about it. Then he shook his head. "Not interested."

He tried to kick my foot away but I grabbed the edge of the door and held on. "Three grand. That's far more than the going rate for border collies."

"Look, lady moneybags. This dog is not for sale. End of story." He pulled so hard on the door that it broke two of my nails. "Now go wave your bills at some other sucker who doesn't know the true value of man's best friend."

I still held the door and pressed my face closer to the crack. "You treat your best friend like crap, Mr. Roxton. He's starving, filthy and covered in flea bites."

He brought his own face close to the opening and his breath smelled like stale coffee and staler booze. "That sounds like a whole lot of mind your own business, babe."

Jilly made a little choking sound. It had been a long time since anyone had called me babe.

"This is an emotional topic," she said, pulling me back from the face-off. "But let's try to be reasonable. My friend is making you a very handsome offer. You seem like an intelligent man—"

"Intelligent enough to know bull crap when I hear it. So save it, toots, and get off my porch."

He reached for something inside and raised it. A baseball bat.

"I'm making one last offer," I said. "Five grand."

Waving the bat, he pushed the door open. "Babe, you just struck out."

CHAPTER THREE

"Well, that's it, then," Jilly said, as we walked down the street so quickly her heels clicked a loud staccato.

"Yes, that's it, then," I said. "I'm going to have to steal the dog."

"Slow down, Ivy. I'm less help to you if I sprain my ankle."

I took a deep breath and slowed. "Okay. But you're not changing my mind."

"I want to rescue the dog with the least possible risk. Let's have a coffee and talk this through."

I agreed reluctantly, and it took five minutes with a hot cup of coffee for steam to stop trickling from my ears. Finally I said, "What kind of guy turns down five grand for a scraggly pup? It doesn't look like he's loaded."

"Hardly." Jilly shook a packet of sugar into her coffee and stirred. "I think it was just belligerence. He didn't like us and didn't want to give in."

"Money usually trumps pride, doesn't it?" I took another sip of my coffee, grateful now for the comforting heat it offered. The day was quite warm for June but I had a chill. "He's hiding something, I can sense it."

"If he wanted to hide something, wouldn't he choose a breed like a rottweiler? A border collie doesn't offer protection."

I stirred my coffee thoughtfully. "Power breeds need proper training and handling and he doesn't seem inclined. Left to its own devices, a dog like that would cause problems with neighbors. Animal Services said no one but me had complained about poor little Keats, the innocuous border collie. He doesn't even bark."

Jilly rubbed away lipstick from her mug and then applied more to her lips. Unlike me, she never needed a mirror to get it just right. "So what's next?"

"Reconnaissance. We go back down the alley and hide in the vacant garage across from the yard. We wait till the guy's gone and then I go over the fence and grab the dog." I wiped my hands together briskly. "Done."

"Done except for whatever he decides to do next."

"What's he going to do, call the police?" I gave her a defiant stare. "If he does, good."

Jilly shook her head. "Guys like him probably don't call the police. Like you said, it seems like he's got something to hide, and that means he's more likely to take care of the problem himself. With his baseball bat."

"He'd have to find me first." It was false bravado and the twitch of her lips said she knew it.

"That probably wouldn't be too hard, since you're going to have to walk the dog and you only live a few blocks away. And then what? He breaks in? Attacks you in a park?"

"I can take care of myself. I have pepper spray."

Ignoring that, she continued. "So then he takes the dog back and poor Keats is worse off than before. Maybe he's locked in the basement for the rest of his days."

My eyes filled instantly and spilled over, rolling down my cheeks and into my coffee cup. "Don't even say that."

"Ivy." She reached across the table and grabbed my hand. "I'm sorry. In all our years of friendship, I've never seen you cry."

"Daisy says they stitched my tear ducts shut at birth. As the last of six, tears weren't going to take me far." I looked up at the ceiling and waited for the emotion to subside. "This dog's broken something in me, Jilly."

"Actually, Flordale did that," she said. "I should have gotten you out years ago, when Wilf came on board. The job's eroded your sense of self ever since." She got up and gathered her things. "We're going to find work that builds you up rather than tears you down. You're so gifted, Ivy. So full of honour and integrity."

That just made me cry again and I dabbed at my eyes with a napkin. I should have skipped the makeup today, but mascara and eyeliner felt like part of my armor against the world. Tears had never been an issue before.

Half an hour later, we skulked down the alley again. Watching Jilly try to be unobtrusive dried my tears and made me smile. We found refuge in the abandoned garage, which smelled of moss, urine and animal dung. Jilly made a gagging sound and pulled a silk scarf out of her purse. She covered her nose like a classy bandit.

We lurked there for more than an hour, watching the house. At first Keats stared in our direction, but I signalled for him to lie down and he collapsed on his side, listless in the heat.

Finally, Ron Roxton came out the side door and unlocked the gate to walk into the yard. He didn't call the dog and though Keats stood, he didn't go over. In fact, he sank to his belly, watching anxiously as his owner circled the yard. Ron stopped to survey the sunflowers for a long moment, and then continued his rounds.

Jilly reached out and squeezed my hand, either to comfort me or hold me in place.

When he found the new bowls I'd left, Ron picked them up and hurled them over the fence, where they landed with a clatter that made Keats cringe even more. After scanning thoroughly with his piggy eyes,

Ron finally walked back out and locked the gate. Then he got into his battered old red Chevy, pulled out and drove away.

"Come on," I said, running down the lane after him. "Let's try to follow him."

"Follow him? Why?" Jilly said. "That wasn't in the plan."

"Maybe we'll learn what he's hiding so we can turn it against him."

She grumbled, but one flick of her red nails got us a cab, and the driver was happy enough to try to tail the red car. The roar of the Chevy's muffler let us know we weren't far behind.

Ten minutes later, the Chevy pulled into a parking lot. By the time we'd paid the cab and got out, Ron Roxton had gone inside the building.

"Now what?" Jilly asked.

"We go in after him. Keep a low profile. See what he's doing."

"Keep a low profile?" Jilly pointed to a neon sign with a flashing profile of a very busty woman. "Ivy, this is a strip club."

"Oh. Well, that's not ideal," I said. "The Booby Trap? How clever."

"It's no big surprise he's the kind of guy who'd spend Saturday afternoon at a strip club, is it?"

"No surprise at all," I said. "Well, I've never been in a strip club, but there's a first time for everything."

Jilly laughed. "No way am I going into a strip club. What exactly did you hope to accomplish from following this guy anyway?"

"Like I said, it's reconnaissance. If we can figure out what he's hiding, maybe we can bring in the police. That way he'd have to surrender Keats, and couldn't replace him with another dog to abuse."

"We're not going to blend in at the Booby Trap, my friend. Next idea?"

"I can blend in almost anywhere," I said. "Let's just go in for a look. See what he's doing."

"We already know what he's doing. Drinking and ogling."

"But others might know him. We can ask questions. That's what we do."

"Ivy, seriously. This is going nowhere good."

I towed her toward the door. "Just one little peek."

"There's no such thing as a little peek at a strip club. It's pretty much the whole enchilada."

It turned out we'd worried for nothing. No sooner had we entered the dark enclave than a beefy young man with a shaved head came to the door. "Hello, ladies. I'm guessing you're in the wrong place this afternoon."

"We—uh—thought we might have a cup of coffee," Jilly said.

"Coffee? Well, there's half a dozen cafés down the street with a view you'd like better."

"Okay, we're here on a dare," I said. "Our friends said we'd never last half an hour."

I tried to peer around him and caught sight of a woman wearing nothing but silver pasties and matching platform heels as she gyrated around a pole. The bouncer moved to block me. "How about I just write you a note to say you did?"

"Are you saying we can't even stay for a drink?" I asked. "That's discrimination."

He offered a surprisingly pleasant smile. "You can stay. I just want you to think twice about it. Your presence could be... distracting... for our regular customers."

Jilly had already backed against the door, but I persisted. "You seem like a nice man. Maybe I could just be honest."

"Best policy," he said. "Not used often enough around this establishment."

"There's this guy," I began.

He held up his hand. "Wait, let me guess. You want to know if your boyfriend is here. You're afraid he's a lowlife cheater."

"We *are* looking for a lowlife. You got that part right," I said. "But the guy in question is an animal abuser. We offered him very good money to buy a dog he's mistreating and he wouldn't take it. So now we're curious about him."

The bouncer crossed his arms and frowned. "I don't like the sounds of this. I have a dog myself. Who's the guy?"

I gave him Ron's name and he nodded. "Small and mean? Sitting at the bar right now?"

Leaning around him, I confirmed it. "He turned down five grand for a border collie he starves and ignores. Doesn't make sense."

"Ladies, I know this guy well enough to warn you away from him. He goes by the nickname Skint and he's got his fingers in plenty of trouble."

"Money making trouble?" I said. "So much that he can turn down five grand?"

"I wouldn't have thought so," he said. "The dog must have value to him."

"Well, it's not like this Skint has sheep to herd," I said. "And this pup couldn't protect him."

The bouncer sighed. "What's your name?"

"Ivy," I said. "And this is Jilly. We're not normally the type to invite trouble with people like Skint."

"I'm Jason. And I could tell." He smiled again. "You're 'Suits' in Saturday casual."

"Pretty much," I said, grinning. "I came upon the dog by accident yesterday but it felt like... well, like fate. It was love at first pat." Tears filled my eyes for the second time that day. "But if I steal the dog I'm afraid this guy will come after me."

He gave a quick nod. "He will, and he's no gentleman. I've had to escort him out a few times for taking liberties with our ladies."

"See, Ivy?" Jilly said. "He's dangerous."

The bouncer gave an uneasy sigh. "Skint's on the wrong side of the wrong people and from what I've heard, he's lucky to be alive right now. So your best bet is to leave well enough alone."

"Jason, a starving, neglected dog is not 'well enough,'" I said. "I just can't leave that alone."

"You've tried Animal Services?"

I nodded. "Useless. And if I keep coming and feeding the dog, Skint will catch me anyway. Maybe he'll move the dog inside so I can't help."

Jason ran one hand over his shaved scalp. "Something tells me I'm going to regret this, but how about I get Skint to talk about his dog and then offer to take it off his hands? I can tell him that my dog needs a friend. If it worked, you could have him."

I reached out and grabbed his hand. "Thank you. Thank you."

Jilly took his other hand. "You are a true gentleman."

"Don't thank me yet, ladies. It's a long shot. But maybe I can figure out why he wants this dog so badly, at least."

I made a move to hug him and he fended me off. "You're amazing," I said. "I don't understand why you're working—"

"In a place like this?" he interrupted, grinning. "I'm in college and it pays better than a coffee shop."

"When you're ready for a new job, we can help," Jilly said, slipping her card into his hand.

"Jason!" There was a shout behind him and I took a step back as I recognized the voice. "Who are you hiding there, big buddy? I see blonde hair."

"Go," Jason said, opening the door and pushing us out. Before it closed behind us, we heard him shout, "It's just two gals looking for a cheating boyfriend. I covered for you, Skint."

As we walked through the parking lot, I said, "I totally want to slash his tires." I peered into the red Chevy. "Look at that. A baseball bat in plain view. As if anyone would believe he's an athlete."

"Come on, slugger," Jilly said. "We need to give Jason time to work his charms. He's the best chance you've got."

My shoulders slumped as I followed her. "I hate leaving my fate—or Keats' fate—in someone else's hands. If this doesn't work, I have a plan B."

On the sidewalk, I raised my hand and a cab zoomed by.

"Yeah, what's that?" Jilly raised *her* hand, and a cab screeched to a stop in seconds, like always.

"I grab the dog and move out of my condo the same day. Take him home to Clover Grove. Skint would never find me there."

She opened the door and gestured for me to slide inside. "You said you'd die before moving back home."

I twisted my hair into a ponytail and smiled. "Times have changed. You can headhunt me a job in the feed store."

Closing the door, she gave the driver the address of Earthy Pleasures, our favourite vegan café and one of the few restaurants that lived up to Jilly's exacting standards. She watched the streets whiz by, before saying, "I hadn't realized how dull our lives had become."

"You're right. Everything feels different now. Goodbye routine."

"Hello, danger," Jilly said, bracing herself as the cab took a turn too fast. "Let's hope we survive the change."

CHAPTER FOUR

I didn't know Jilly even owned old jeans but she'd dug out a pair, along with a dark chambray shirt and sneakers for our stakeout the next afternoon. Her bright hair was under a black baseball cap. Turned out you could disguise a sunflower, after all. Today she was no more than an average daisy, of which there were many in Skint's yard, too, along with tiger lilies.

"You wouldn't expect Skint to be interested in gardening, would you?" I asked, accepting a paper cup of coffee she poured from a thermos. Sitting cross-legged on cardboard that protected us from the damp earth in the rundown garage, we waited for Skint to leave so we could feed Keats and spend a bit of time with him. I'd managed to find a vet to dispense flea and tick medications and was eager to get the pup treated so he'd stop scratching his skin raw.

"I'm sure Skint didn't plant those flowers," she said, smoothing her jeans. "My guess is he's renting anyway."

Jason, the bouncer, had texted Jilly the night before saying Skint had shot down the dog conversation, but he'd keep trying. He said he'd have plenty of chances because Skint was a regular at the Booby Trap, normally arriving on weekends by three, and weekdays by six. That gave us an idea of when the coast would be clear to care for Keats. My anxiety reduced by half just hearing that. At least I could get the dog healthy while I figured out how to free him.

"I'll have to leave work early to see him," I said. "Even at this time of year the alley is dark and creepy in the evening."

She gave me a sharp glance. "You say that as if you know it for fact."

"Well, I popped by last night, if you must know."

"Actually, yeah, I must know what you're doing in a dangerous alley at night, Ivy. Just like we text each other when we're on dates to be safe."

"You mean *you* text *me* when you're on dates. I haven't been on a date in recent memory."

"That's because you left your heart in Clover Grove." She continued to direct her intense green stare at me. "Maybe that's why you want to go home all of a sudden? To see that high school sweetheart you won't talk about. Although we supposedly tell each other everything."

"You know almost everything worth telling about my boring youth." I broke off a piece of the scone she'd baked that morning. "Some ghosts are better left at rest."

"Okay, fine, but I hope you realize that the more time we spend on stakeout, the more I'll probe these dark corners of your memory." She took a bite of the scone, chewed, and then examined the chunk in her hand with evident disgust. "Sawdust. This confirms I'm a cook, not a baker."

"Tastes delicious to me. You underestimate your talent."

She shook her head. "I have talent for cooking, not baking. Bakers are rule-followers and I prefer freestyle. Give me some chicken, tomato, basil and cheese, and I can build you a dream. But today we needed something highly portable. Stakeout grub."

I wolfed down another chunk and mumbled, "Thank you. For everything, Jilly. You're the best friend ever."

"True." Her smile couldn't be dimmed even with camouflage and dingy surroundings. "Just to hit rewind for a second, I'm pretty sure you mentioned going to work. Does that mean you're not quitting Flordale?"

I heaved a sigh that blew scone crumbs around. The raccoons would be glad to collect them later. "It means I've calmed down enough to listen to you. Since I'm not sure what I want to do next, it makes sense to keep my options open. Drama never helped anyone. So, I'll go in and suck up to Wilf tomorrow."

"Wise decision, my friend." Her relief was palpable. "I'll work my database to start generating leads."

Plucking blueberries out of the scone, I ate them one by one. "My dream job probably isn't in your database. I think I'm done with HR. I just need to figure out my next life."

"Patience. It sounds like you're having a midlife crisis at thirty-three."

"Maybe." I peered out of the garage and then jerked back. Skint was standing across the yard by the gate. Keats had stretched to the end of his chain to press against the wire fence closest to us. I'd have to discourage that, as it would give away our hiding spot.

Jilly grabbed my hand and we held our breath, waiting. Finally we released it as we heard the car door close, and then the roar of the red Chevy. After the racket faded away, we got up. Both of us had stiffened and shook our legs to loosen up.

When I walked to the fence, Keats went a little crazy from joy, offering an array of tricks I knew Skint had never taught him. He stood on his hind legs, spun in a pirouette, rolled over, offered a paw and then spontaneously leapt into the air like a breaching whale.

"Wow," Jilly said. "That was a full circus performance in less than a minute."

"He's a genius," I said. "Now, boost me over."

"Boost you...?" Her jaw dropped open. "Excuse me. You must be thinking of another friend. Like Jason the bouncer, perhaps. Jilly Black-wood doesn't do manual labor."

"Fine." I stuck my sneaker through the wire. "If I break my leg, you get to deal with Skint."

"You grew up in farm country. I'm sure climbing comes naturally to you."

"I grew up in a small bungalow where we were stacked on top of each other. Five girls in one room, and when I finally got the top bunk, I fell out a lot. Asher, my brother, got his own room."

"Still bitter?" she asked.

"Kind of, yeah. I still can't believe he's a cop in Clover Grove, since he was a rather skilled shoplifter as a kid. He kept us from scurvy since fruit was his speciality."

Jilly laughed as I leapt from the top of the fence. "Something tells me you got up to some shady business yourself, Ivy."

I grinned at her as I fought Keats off. "I drove getaway. On a bike."

Picking up the dog, I hugged him. As if by magic, my heartbeat and breathing slowed. The cuddle didn't last long, however. Like all border collies—even malnourished ones—Keats had energy to spare.

"It's okay, buddy," I said, setting him down. "I know you're pent up. Chaining a herding dog is tantamount to torture."

"Snuggling isn't a great idea until the meds have a chance to work, anyway," Jilly said. "He's covered in fleas. The yard must be hopping with them."

I took my bag of supplies from her and gave him the medications. Then I poured a large serving of high-end vet food into the bowls we'd collected from the alley. The kibble disappeared in a flash, and then he drank from the other bowl.

Examining the dog's collar, I gasped. "Skint's put a tiny lock on the dog's collar and tightened it so that it can't slip over his head. It's practically cutting into his skin."

Jilly gasped, too. "That's new?"

I nodded sadly. "You were right. Keats is paying the price for my behavior."

"I didn't want to be right." Her voice was barely a whisper. "We'll need bolt cutters to free him."

"I'd like to cut Skint's bolts." Standing, I looked around. "Do you think he's hiding something back here? Remember how he circled the yard and lingered by the garden?"

"I think you need to get out right now. Because if he catches you inside his yard, we may not have such easy access to Keats. The dog is better off where we can at least feed him."

It was all I could do to stop myself from exploring, but I didn't want Keats to suffer more because of my curiosity.

After handing the bag back to Jilly, I bent to kiss Keats on the top of his head. Despite the conditions, he smelled oddly sweet, like grass and clover. "See you tomorrow, buddy."

Keats picked up one of the bowls and offered it to me. When I took it, he picked up the other. I handed them both to Jilly. "He really is smart," she said.

One of my sneakers was in the fence when I heard the roar of the Chevy in the distance. My heart zoomed into overdrive. "Uh-oh."

"He's coming," Jilly said. "Hurry hurry hurry."

My limbs seemed to lose all coordination. My arms felt like jelly and my legs didn't get the message to climb. I managed to pull myself to the top of the fence but then I lost my balance and fell backwards into the yard. Keats climbed onto my chest as if to disguise me.

"Hide," I told Jilly. "Garage. Now."

She did as she was told, protesting all the way.

Meanwhile the Chevy pulled into the driveway and the door creaked open and then slammed shut. There was a long pause during which I played dead and prayed. But finally the gate to the yard rattled and Skint shouted, "I see you, Suit. Get out from under my dog right now."

I shoved Keats off gently and got up. "Oh, hi, Mr. Roxton. How are you today?"

"Skip the small talk. I told you to stay away from my dog. And now you're in my yard with my dog. I could shoot you, you know."

My blood seemed to chill in my veins at the thought of a gun. But if there was one thing I'd learned in HR, it was to mask my feelings. I'd forgotten how on Friday but my skills seemed to be functioning more normally today.

"Is it legal to own a firearm in Boston?" I asked.

"It's always legal to shoot someone trying to burglarize your property."

"Feeding your dog isn't burglary, is it?" I reached into my pocket for my phone. "Let's call the cops and get a second opinion."

He crossed the yard in a few bounds and grabbed my wrist. "I wouldn't do that, babe. I really wouldn't."

"And I wouldn't lay a hand on a woman, Mr. Roxton, I really wouldn't." He let go of my arm. "Look, if the cops want me to leave, I'll have them see me out."

His eyes were darting around the yard and they kept going back to the sunflowers. "No cops," he said. "Or else."

"Or else?"

He shrugged simply. "The dog suffers. You want that?"

That was the exact opposite of what I wanted. "What I want is to take the dog and leave your yard forever. It seems like a win-win."

He shook his head and gave me a gap-toothed leer. "I already win, babe. You're trespassing and I don't need a gun to make you leave. There are quieter weapons that don't need a licence."

Like the baseball bat I'd seen in his car.

"Understood," I said. "As a matter of fact, I was just leaving. Would you mind if I used the gate?"

He stepped back to let me pass. I straightened my shoulders and walked as steadily as I could, considering my legs still weren't cooperating. I gave Keats a look that warned him to stay quiet.

"Don't even look at my dog," he said.

I stared at the garden instead. "What gorgeous sunflowers, and they've bloomed so early. You have a real green thumb, Mr. Roxton. What do you use for fertilizer?"

Turning, I saw he'd grown pale. A trickle of sweat ran down his brow. "Like I give a crap about flowers. They were there when I got here. Now shut up and get out."

I walked out of the gate and turned. "It was nice chatting with you again. Would you mind if I sent a horticulturist over to check out your sunflowers? I haven't seen this variety since I was a kid. I think it's an ancient strain and those seeds are like gold today. I bet you could command a good price for them."

"If you send anyone over you know what happens to the dog." He slammed the gate shut behind me. "Got it?"

I rested my arms on the top of the fence and gave him a fake smile. "Got it. I won't even think about sending a horticulturist over as long as I can see the dog is happy and thriving. Every single day. Sound good?"

He flipped me the bird, but the rivulets of sweat had multiplied, telling me I'd hit the bullseye. He was hiding something in the garden and was desperate enough to protect it that he'd strike a deal with me.

"You can look at my dog from outside my fence," he said. "I'll be installing security to make sure you stay out."

I gave him my blandest HR smile. "Deal. I'm glad we had this meeting of minds, today, Mr. Roxton. You're a reasonable man."

"And you're a Suit who needs a reality check. I look forward to giving it to you."

CHAPTER FIVE

W ilf Darby carried himself like a guy who'd been a high school hottie 40 years ago. Time had claimed most of his heat but in his own mind he still had a full head of hair, an angular jawline and a six-pack. It seemed like he expected people to feel grateful for a moment of his attention.

None of this would have bothered me one bit if he'd been a good leader, but our department had dwindled during his reign. The staff that once made up my work family had left for other challenges. Most had given up on Flordale and found greener pastures. Jilly was behind quite a few of those departures. I didn't blame them—or her—but I missed my pals. For the last three years, my former passion had become no more than a job that was sucking the soul out of me.

On Monday morning, I noticed the curious stares as I walked into the office. I'd chosen my best suit—black, lightweight wool cut just right —to shield me from all the eyes. Some were genuinely sympathetic, and those were the eyes I avoided most. Sympathy would only make me feel more vulnerable. I needed to keep up the front and get this day behind me. Tonight I could visit Keats again, and plot our retreat to border collie country.

The message arrived with a ping before I'd even hooked up my laptop at my workstation. Wilf had issued his summons. I put my purse in my bottom drawer and walked to his glass-walled corner office with the spectacular view. Shoulders back, shields up, fake smile firmly in place. There was a dribble of sweat between my shoulder blades but no one could see that.

"Morning, Killer," he said, when I walked in and perched in the chair opposite his desk. He took his time finishing up whatever he was doing on the computer.

"Morning, boss."

I hated it when he called me Killer. It diminished the impact our work had on people—real people who frequently left their final meeting with me in tears. The men were more likely to cry than woman, I'd found, perhaps because their identity was so tied up in their professional lives. They knew how hard it was to find a new job when the downsizing stain appeared on their records. I referred many of them to Jilly, whose small but mighty company had the highest success rate of any headhunter in the city. Seeing them thrive in a new role was good for her, good for the client and balm for my beleaguered soul. I kept a record of those I'd downsized, and what happened afterwards. Jilly told me I got too attached; now I saw the toll that had taken.

When Wilf finally turned, I said, "How was your weekend?"

"Good." He cracked his knuckles and then folded his beefy hands across his belly. His smile was as fake as mine. With glass walls, he needed to keep things clean. "How ya feeling? You looked green around the gills when you left our meeting on Friday. And you didn't answer calls or emails... That's not like you."

"I caught a terrible bug. Down for the count all weekend with a fever. Even now I feel like I could throw up."

His pale blue eyes widened. "Feel free to excuse yourself if that's going to happen."

"For sure. I'm just going to take it easy till all this passes."

"You do that." He leaned back in his chair. "As long as it passes fast."

I folded my hands in my lap. "There's a deadline for flu?"

"Only for you." He waited a beat and then gave a loud guffaw. "Just kidding. But you do know this department can't manage without you, Ivy."

"Aw, that's sweet. But everyone's replaceable. Isn't that what you always say?"

"I never say that." He gave me a wink. "Not on the record, anyway."

"Actually, I agree with you. Sometimes it's best for everyone to part ways."

He gave a little smirk that was more genuine. "Glad you feel that way, Killer. Because that's the attitude you're going to need for the next year."

"The next year?"

"It'll probably take that long to offload Flordale's dead wood around the world. I suggest you travel light. Use carry-on."

"I know the drill," I said, sighing. "It sounds daunting at the moment."

"Must be the flu talking because a challenge never bothered you."

Casting a sideways glance, I confirmed my suspicion that everyone was watching us. "You're right, Wilf. I always did like a challenge."

His smirk faded and his hands stretched out, palms down on the desk. "What's going on, Killer? You've got a chance to see the world on the company dollar. That's how I'd look at it."

"I find travel more tiring than I used to. I'm not as young as I used to be."

He laughed, this time more sincerely. "You're a babe compared to me."

I winced at the word, even though he didn't mean it the way Skint had.

"Killer. Talk to me. You're not yourself." He sounded sympathetic but his eyes were cagey.

"All good. Just tired. I need a few weeks to recover my spark."

"We don't have a few weeks. Sylvia's out there booking your flights now. You leave Wednesday for Paris and you'll be gone for two months."

A little gasp slipped out. "I can't leave so soon."

"Why? What aren't you telling me?" He attempted a grin that didn't meet his eyes. "Have you met someone?"

I pushed the chair back from the desk to allow a quick escape. "How would that happen with the hours I work?"

"True. I've always said you're married to the company. We truly value that dedication, Killer."

"Thank you, Wilf. Then I know you'll understand when I say I need at least two weeks to gear up for this. I'm sure you're joking when you call me Killer, but you must know it takes a toll to fire so many people. Destroy their lives. Have you ever been downsized?"

His already florid face flushed. I knew he'd been let go from a job long ago, but he'd obviously managed to bury those feelings deeply so that he could dehumanize our staff. He even made sure our packages for those we fired were as stingy as possible.

"Let's keep our eyes on the prize, Ivy." I noticed the switch to my real name. "The prize is a healthy company, and right now Flordale needs to trim the fat." He leaned across the desk, all the better to shove me back in line. "You're the fat trimmer. Our very own grim reaper. We can't afford for you to lose your edge now. To get soft."

"Of course not. Understood, sir." I straightened out of my slump and plastered that fake smile back on. "Fear not. You can deploy your weapon of corporate death soon."

There was relief in his sigh. "That sounds more like you."

"All I'm asking is that you push back deployment by two weeks, Wilf. If I fly when I'm so depleted, I could get really sick, and then we'd be in a pickle. I'll do all my preparation here so that I can move even faster overseas."

He turned back to his computer. "I'm afraid there's no flexibility,

Ivy. Visit a doctor to get whatever pharmaceuticals you need to make this happen. You fly Wednesday. That's a direct order."

I stood abruptly and said, "Give me your wastebasket. I'm going to—"

"Run, Killer!" He pushed his seat back and raised his hands. "Run."

CHAPTER SIX

I didn't run. Instead, I kept a nice steady pace as I walked across the workspace and headed outside to grab some fresh air. Then I came back inside and spent the rest of the day cleaning up my files. I knew with sudden clarity that I wouldn't be on a plane to Paris this week, or anytime soon. I'd promised Keats, and I would not abandon him. Even though Jilly had offered to watch over the dog, there was no way I could travel for months and leave her with that responsibility. I was the one who'd made the commitment, and with a man like Skint in charge of Keats, I couldn't put Jilly in danger on her own.

I'd made another decision during my meeting with Wilf: I wouldn't abandon myself, either. After 10 years of so-called marriage to Flordale, they were willing to throw me to the dogs, as it were. If I didn't hop on a plane immediately, I'd very likely top the list of the downsized and Wilf would deliver the news himself. I was well paid for my service, but it was no longer enough. I wanted to treat people like humans; I wanted to be treated like a human myself. That apparently wasn't possible here. Not anymore.

I wished I could stay until I had a soft landing in place, but since Paris was out of the question, I had to make my move immediately.

What I could do was leave my professional house in perfect order. My colleague Keri was the one most likely to take over my work, and I quite liked her. I'd do my best to ease her transition into the deep waters of the Flordale shark tank.

At around 7 p.m., when everyone had left the office, I went through my drawers and files, and packed what I wanted to keep into my bag. I locked the laptop in the drawer and left the key under the mug with the great white shark on it that Wilf had given me when he pulled my name in Secret Santa.

Tomorrow, I'd submit a letter to the vice president requesting to be downsized. I'd earned the buy-out, not only with years of service, but with the long list of grievances, great and small, that I'd recorded about Wilf's behavior. Maybe he'd get a chance to experience downsizing himself again, and this time it might make a lasting impression.

I hoped they'd do the right thing, but if not, I had a nest egg to fall back on, and a condo to sell. It was enough to get a fresh start somewhere else.

The evening was surprisingly warm when I walked out the front door. In fact, a wall of heat hit me, and after a few stifling steps, I stopped and took off my jacket. It wouldn't fit in my bag with everything else, so I dropped it in the nearest trash bin and kept walking. "Suit" no more. Whatever the future held, I probably wouldn't need 15 of them.

My heart lifted as I turned into the first alley and hurried toward my clandestine rendezvous with the tuxedoed male in my life. Mixed with the excitement was fear. What if Skint had locked him inside? What if he'd harmed him in some way to punish me? But a small voice told me I was right about his having something to hide in that yard. Until he got that resolved, Keats was likely safe, but I'd have to make my move soon.

I was practically running by the time I reached the yard and relief surged through me when I saw the black and white creature stretched out on the grass and panting in the sweltering heat. He was on his paws in a second, however, dragging the heavy chain to me as fast as he could.

After making sure the red Chevy was gone and there were no signs of life in the house, I dropped to my knees and let him lick my face through the wire.

"How are you doing, buddy? You hungry?"

He gave a hearty wag that erased some of the cares of my day. Keeping one eye on the house, I poured a baggie of kibble into a foil container I'd brought, and water into another. Despite the weather, the dog's regular water bowl was tipped and empty. He wouldn't last long in a heat wave without me. I poured a large bottle of water into the foil container after he'd eaten and he drank all of it.

After that, he offered me his usual array of tricks with no seeming motive other than to put a smile on my face, which it did.

I pulled a ball out of my bag and said, "Want to learn fetch, canine Einstein?"

He wagged even harder, so I tossed the ball and it rolled into the garden. He ran over to get it, dragging the chain. Picking up the ball, he carried it back and dropped it beside the fence.

The ball wouldn't fit through the wire, and there was no way I could reach it without jumping in. I didn't fancy another confrontation with Skint, so I just said, "That was stupid of me, Keats. I'm sorry."

Keats didn't give up as easily. Instead, he started digging, evidently trying to free the ball so I could grab it underneath.

"Good boy," I said. "Dig. Dig."

In no time there was a hole the perfect size, and he nudged the ball out like a gumball from a machine. I tossed it toward the house, but it arced into the sunflowers again. Keats fetched it back and released the ball into the trough.

I sent Jilly a video of him fetching the ball and dropping it under the fence and she called me immediately.

"That dog's Mensa material," she said.

"What if I helped him to dig himself out to freedom?" I asked.

"I think Mr. Skint would still come after you. We need a better plan."

"But in the meantime, Keats is going to fry out here." I waited a beat and added, "At least I'll be able to get over here more often to make sure he has water."

"Oh yeah?" Her tone shot to red alert. "How so?"

"I'm quitting Flordale tomorrow." She started to speak and I talked over her. "Wilf insisted on sending me to Paris on Wednesday, even though I begged for a couple of weeks. I told him I wasn't feeling well, which was true, and he advised me to pick up meds and get packing. As a dutiful wife to the company."

"What an idiot," Jilly said. "Okay. Get a good night's sleep and we'll meet for an early breakfast and strategize."

Relief flooded through me again when she didn't fight my decision. "How about meeting for a drink tonight instead?"

"Even better." I heard her heels clicking as she started to get ready. It was a rare evening that I offered to go out.

"Can you bring me a sweater? I threw out my suit jacket in a flagrant statement as I left the office. But the bar will probably be pumping A/C."

She laughed. "Keep your pants on, okay? Otherwise the only bar that will serve us is the Booby Trap."

While we chatted, Keats had gone over to the garden and started digging there, too. The dirt flew up from his snowy paws. "Leave it, Keats," I called. "Skint will have our heads if you dig up his rare sunflowers."

The dog wagged his white-tipped tail and mumbled a story. He sounded excited.

"What's he saying?" Jilly asked. "Have you cracked the code yet?"

"Sounds like another tall tale," I said. "Tail... get it?"

"Wine might improve your puns."

I threw the ball again to distract Keats. It soared up, bright orange against the peachy sunset sky, and then landed in the sunflowers again. No matter how hard I tried to aim differently, it kept landing there. I'd always been a disaster at sports, and the company baseball league had discreetly fired me.

Keats bounded after it with a jangle of metal and more dirt flew.

"He's found another ball," I said, getting to my feet and peering over the fence. "It's big. He's rolling it with his nose." I aimed the phone at him and filmed it for Jilly. "I hope Skint doesn't freak out at the mess."

The dog rolled the big ball against the fence and I gave a little shriek.

"Ow. I needed that ear," Jilly said. "What happened?"

My fingers shook as I hit send on the video. "It's not a ball, Jilly. Check your phone."

There was silence on the other end and then a scream even louder than mine. "Oh my god. Is that what I think it is?"

"Only if you think it's a skull."

"Why is Keats rolling a skull around?"

"He unearthed it from the sunflowers. Maybe the rest of the skeleton is in the garden, too. Now we know what Skint's been hiding."

"Ivy, get out of there, fast. When Skint gets home and finds that skull, he'll use his baseball bat on yours."

I squared my shoulders. "I'm not leaving Keats with a murderer. I'm stealing him right now."

"Don't, Ivy, please. Wait till I get there."

"I'm done waiting. Skint could show up randomly like he did yesterday."

"Call the cops before you end up the next body under the sunflowers."

"There are worse places to rest, I guess." I stuck my foot in the chain link.

"Then I'll call the cops while you get the dog and the skull."

"Deal," I said. "I'm going to put the phone in my pocket. Meet me at my place in 20 minutes, K?"

The phone was still in my hand when I heard the sound of a blown muffler heading our way. I cursed softly, trying to think.

"Ivy? Talk to me. What's happening?"

"He's coming. I hear the car. And the skull's lying beside the fence."

"Okay, stay calm. Gather up everything you can and run to the garage. Send Keats to the gate so that there's no reason for Skint to come that far."

"Good idea. But I've got a better one." Dropping the phone in my pocket, I said, "Keats, dig. Now." He started enlarging the hole on his side and I did the same on mine. In less than a minute, there was a deep enough opening and he nudged the skull under the fence. I pulled it through and then shoved it aside, muttering, "Sorry. Sorry." Quickly I filled in as much of the hole as I could. Then I stood and gathered everything up. Clutching the skull against my belly, I shuddered. "*It's just a dirty old ball,*" I told myself as I ran to the garage. Turning at the door, I said, "Keats, go."

I moved inside just seconds before the Chevy's lights poured into the yard. Backing against the wall, I jumped when I heard scrabbling sounds overhead. If a raccoon landed on me now, I'd scream. I might drop the skull first, and then scream.

"What's going on?" Jilly's voice was tinny and faraway in my pocket.

The car lights went off and I leaned out. I could see Keats standing by the gate. Skint walked over and peered into the yard.

"Keats is performing," I whispered, pulling back. "He's on his hind legs, dancing and spinning like a robot on crack. If I didn't know better I'd say he's distracting Skint."

I poked my head out again to see Skint leaning on the fence staring at the dog as if he'd never seen him before. He probably *hadn't* seen this remarkable circus act. Keats went through his whole repertoire of tricks, more than I'd seen. I held my breath and even the critters in the rafters above me settled down. The evening was eerily quiet.

Finally, Skint shook his head and said, "Guess you're not as stupid as I thought." He sounded mystified. After nearly a minute passed, during which I was pretty sure I was going to faint, he unlocked the gate to the yard. "I'm taking you down to Boobies. There's a guy there who likes dogs and I think Misty, the dancer, does too. You can show them your tricks. Maybe I'll get a free drink out of it. Or better."

He gave a sleazy laugh as he walked across the grass to free the chain from the tree. It wasn't far from the site of the excavation. As if to keep up the distraction, Keats cavorted along by his side, acting the clown.

"You settle down," Skint said. "Save your energy for your circus act. This is a one-time deal. Play the fool and you might not make it back home."

He coiled the long chain around his tattooed arm, then pulled the small dog behind him to the Chevy and opened the back door. Keats didn't jump in voluntarily, so Skint bent and hoisted him in none too gently.

"What's happening now?" Jilly whispered.

"He's taking Keats down to the bar to impress Jason and a stripper."

"Okay. Okay. Well, if he thinks Keats is going to get him some stripper love, he won't hurt him, right?"

I waited till Skint had locked the gate and left in the car before I answered. "He also said that Keats might not make it back home if he didn't perform on command." When I was sure the coast was clear, I stepped out and started walking. "I can't take a chance on that, so I'm heading down to the Booby Trap now. Meet me there?"

"No freakin' way." Jilly's voice was now loud and clear. "We've got to call the cops right now about that skull."

"Right. The skull." I dropped the phone into my pocket again and went back into the garage. My bag was full, so I dumped my things from the office in the corner. Then I shoved the skull into my bag and covered it with the Team Flordale baseball cap I'd kept in a prescient moment of sentiment.

Then I started walking, wiping my hands on my black pants. They were so caked in grime there was no hope.

"I'm waiting," Jilly called from my pocket.

"I know, I know." I groped for the phone. "I'm going to grab a cab now."

"Ivy Galloway, you get back in the garage with that skull and stay there until the cops arrive. You cannot go down to that strip bar on your own and confront a murderer with grizzly evidence."

"He's not going to know I have the skull in my purse. It's a big bag."

"It's in your purse?" She gave a long groan. "You know exactly what's going to happen, don't you? It's going to fall out because you're accident prone. And then what?"

I was already in front of Skint's house looking down the road for a cab. Hopefully for once, I could manage to flag one without my eye-catching friend at my side.

"I promise I will not drop the skull. I'll call the police now and head over to keep an eye on Skint. Do you want to come here and talk to the police or meet me at the bar?"

"Of course I'm coming to the bar. I'd never leave you to deal with a murderer alone." I heard street noise and honking. "Okay, I got a cab."

It figured. I was still waving frantically and three had passed me. "Traffic is awful. I hope Keats is all right," I said, walking toward a busier intersection.

"What's the plan, exactly?" Jilly asked.

"All I know for the moment is that I have to keep a good grip on my bag." Finally a cab stopped and I jumped in. "It's a shame because I've always liked this bag and now I'll never be able to use it again."

CHAPTER SEVEN

I could have walked to the bar faster. Every block felt like torture as I fretted about what was happening down at the Booby Trap. Jilly was stuck in a gridlock, too, and she had a lot more distance to cover. Finally she hung up to call the police. Meanwhile, I sweltered in what was probably the only cab in the city with broken air conditioning. Normally I wouldn't mind so much, but anxiety had pushed my core temperature into the red an hour ago.

When I couldn't take it anymore, I paid the driver and got out. The sidewalks were packed with people out enjoying the first summery evening. I wove through the foot traffic as quickly as I could, keeping my bag pressed tightly to my side. Jilly was right: I *was* accident prone. That's why Flordale's baseball team gave me a cap and eased me onto the sidelines. Yet here I was practically running down a busy street with someone's head joggling under my arm.

Someone's head. I didn't want to think about it. I only wanted to focus on Keats, my sweet pup, but it was hard to drive the image out of my mind. The skull had been under the sunflowers for years, it would seem, because it didn't smell.

Or did it? I raised my right hand to my nose and caught only a whiff of damp soil. That moment of distraction was my undoing. Suddenly I tripped on what was probably a small crack but felt like a huge fissure. Then I was down. I rolled at least once, but somehow I managed to clutch my bag. That meant I only had one hand to brace my fall and I lost a layer of skin in the process.

"Are you all right?" A man leaned over to help me up and I flinched.

"Don't touch me."

"I just wanted to—"

"I know. I'm sorry. Thank you." *It's just that I have a skull in my purse and I don't want you to see it.* "I'm fine, really. Just a scratch or two."

Springing to my feet, I started a brisk trot again, paying more attention. That was a close call. A really close call. If the skull had rolled into traffic, I could end up in custody myself. Not only that, it was a desecration. I owed it to the owner of that skull to slow down.

Keats would likely be fine. He'd do his tricks and Jason would protect him. There was probably a crowd in the parking lot right now applauding.

But when I finally reached the Booby Trap, there was no one in sight. Worse, Skint's car wasn't out front like I expected. Picking up speed, I careened around the corner of the building. All I could see was a large dumpster down the lane. I'd have to circle the entire building. He must be around here somewhere.

When I reached the dumpster, however, my search ended. Skint had backed the red Chevy in beside it so that the car was invisible from the front of the bar.

Why would he park all the way down there? Unless he had something to hide.

"Oh no oh no oh no," I moaned. "He wouldn't."

But he had. Keats was spread out on the back seat during what was surely a record-breaking day for heat. The windows were closed and the dog appeared to be unconscious.

"Keats," I said, rapping hard on the window. "Wake up. Are you okay?"

The dog didn't move, but I sensed that he was still aware... that his spirit was strong. Tears poured down my face as I pressed my nose to the glass. Finally, one white paw gave the slightest twitch.

"Hang on, buddy. I'll get you out. I promise."

CHAPTER EIGHT

Pushing myself off the car, I ran through my options. I could call the cops and wait for them to force their way through the traffic jam. That was the right thing to do, but there would be so many competing calls tonight, and a trapped dog probably wouldn't be high on their list. I could call Animal Services, but they'd also be under siege in this heat. Last, I could charge into the bar and take on Skint myself, letting peer pressure force him to release Keats. But the dog would need veterinary attention and was unlikely to get it with Skint. And I'd still be left dealing with him later.

Or I could take matters into my own hands. Jilly had called the police anyway. At this point, every second counted and Keats was slipping further away from me.

I wanted to sit down right there and cry, but I couldn't. He was only in this predicament because of me. If I hadn't formed a bond with him, he wouldn't have commanded his owner's attention and ended up getting heat stroke outside a strip bar.

Well, there was no time for tears, and the game wasn't over yet.

First thing I did was text Jilly quickly. Then I put the phone away and started looking for something to break into the car. A piece of piping, perhaps, or a heavy log. Even a wooden crate from the bar might work, if I hit the window just right. I wasn't particularly strong, but I did have fury on my side.

The dumpster was so close and so tall that I overlooked it at first. Then I backed right up and tipped my head. It was full to overflowing and all kinds of possibilities poked out of the pile.

I slipped around the back of it and stowed my bag in the deepening shadows. Then I returned to the side of the red car and began to climb.

It was more of a nail-breaking scrabble. There were two slim rungs that didn't provide much purchase for my work loafers with their smooth leather soles. The metal was slippery, despite a coating of rust.

"Spiderman makes this look so easy," I muttered, inching my way up the side. It was really only about a five-foot climb to the top but it might as well have been Everest.

Finally I got one hand over the top and then it was smooth sailing. My upper body strength wasn't impressive but the fuel of panic made tipping into the bin surprisingly easy.

Being *inside* the dumpster was no picnic, however. All the refuse from the past week was rotting in the heat. Plastic bags had been torn open by the local raccoons for a feast on bar grub. There was a sudden rustle and three rats popped out of the garbage and ran up and over the side with an agility that both repelled and amazed me.

There was no time to think about putrid horrors. I needed a good, solid weapon right now. Below me, my new best friend's life force was slipping away.

I scanned the heap and there it was, standing in relief against the sunset sky. It was like a magical weapon from an ancient fantasy, only in the form of a common baseball bat.

Since it was pretty close to the red Chevy's driver's seat, I guessed this was the same baseball bat Skint had threatened me with at his front door. The same baseball bat that had been in the back seat of his car the next day. Why he'd pitch it into the trash was beyond me. But there it was, and I was going to use it against him.

The 12-foot crossing was the most disgusting experience of my life. I clung to the side as if my life depended on it. Maybe it did. There was a chance I could sink into oblivion in decomposing bar trash that wouldn't hold my weight. What a sad way to go, smothered under week-old chicken wings and nachos.

I scrambled through fetid, squishy bags, almost doing the breaststroke at one point, until I reached the baseball bat. Grabbing it, I managed to hoist myself up on the lip of the dumpster and looked down on the car. It would be simpler going down, but not easy. First, I leaned over as far as I could and dropped the bat. It rolled under the car and I cursed. I didn't need another challenge, another delay.

Turning on the edge was tough, too, because my hands already ached from my fall and subsequent climb, and now they were covered in garbage slime. I managed to turn and lower myself over the side till I was hanging. Then it was only a yard or so to drop to the pavement. Still, when I let go it felt like the world was slipping away and there was a sudden jolt as my feet hit the pavement. I lost my balance and fell beside the car.

On the bright side, I could see the baseball bat, and with a bit of squirming and stretching, it was in my hand.

Scrambling back, I got to my feet. There was no time to lament the loafer I'd lost in the trash. I needed to assess my strategy. Keats was in the same position, with his head near the passenger door on the opposite side. The best way to minimize his glass shower was to whack the driver's window. Luckily, Skint had left plenty of room between the car and the dumpster for me to get a good swing.

I held up the bat and discovered why he'd disposed of it: there was a crack running down the middle. A wave of nausea hit me. How had he cracked it? And did it still have the integrity to do the job? I wasn't sure I had the strength to go back up into the bin, and judging by the sweat pouring down my face from the effort, Keats wouldn't have long inside the car, either.

It *had* to do the job. But I would only have one chance before it broke apart.

I wiped each hand in turn on my pants to get rid of as much sweat and garbage juice as possible. Now I could get a good grip.

"Keats, stay calm," I said. "There's going to be a scary noise but then you'll be free. Forever."

I got into position, bringing the bat back just like they taught me on the Flordale baseball team before they cut me. Today, however, I liked the feeling of the bat in my hands. I felt powerful, rather than powerless. No one would laugh at me now.

Besides, the target was considerably bigger and stationary.

"One... two... three." It seemed like everything dropped into slow motion after that. There was the smooth arc of the swing. The perfect landing of the bat in the center of the window. The smash and spiderweb of cracks before the glass completely shattered.

I hadn't expected it to be so loud but it was enough to make my ears ring. Inside the bar, the music would surely muffle the boom and the tinkling of the glass falling away.

At any rate, I didn't have time to lose. The baseball bat had fractured from impact, leaving me holding a stub. There was enough of it left to clear some of the remaining glass. I reached inside and unlatched the passenger door on my side. Then I dropped the stub and lifted Keats. His body was limp and his eyes closed as I carried him away from the glass, careful to avoid the worst of it myself, given my missing shoe. The long chain dragged behind me with an ominous rattle.

Setting the dog on the warm pavement, I went to get my purse. Under the skull was a bottle of water. Thank god I hadn't dumped that in my frenzy to accommodate my guest.

Kneeling beside him, I pried open the dog's jaws and poured a little water inside. After a second or two, his tongue moved and I started crying again as I poured in a little more. His blue eye opened just a slit and seemed to glow in the fading light.

"I have to get you to a vet, buddy," I said. "That means carrying you down this alley and right in front of the bar doors. In case you haven't noticed, I'm covered in filth and I have a hard time hailing a cab at the best of times. So this isn't going to be easy. Drink what you can now."

A minute or two later, he lifted his head, sniffed and whined.

"Yeah, you're right," I said standing. "We've gotta get out of here. Just let me grab the skull."

The blue eye looked up at me again, wider now.

"Long story," I said, turning to bend over my bag. "Bringing it along seemed like the right thing to do."

It wasn't, however. Bringing the skull along had been exactly the wrong thing to do.

CHAPTER NINE

Y ou don't really appreciate air until you have none of it left. As I stooped over my bag and shoved things around inside, someone slipped a loop of chain link around my neck and tightened it. Instantly, I dropped the bag and the skull rolled out. My hands went to the chain—Keats' leash—and pried at it.

"You shouldn't have brung that," Skint said, his breath hot on my ear.

Well, I knew that now but it was a little late. The skull was going to be the last thing I saw as I suffocated behind a dumpster. There was no doubt in my mind that Skint would haul me up and over and leave my body among the chicken wings and nachos. The rats would have a field day.

It played out in my mind like a short film as I struggled. The last frame was an aerial shot of me splayed out, eyes staring sightlessly at the sky from the junk pile with the little black and white dog curled by my side.

Keats.

No.

This man was not going to end my dog and leave *him* to the rats.

I swung around hard and kicked Skint in the gut with my work loafer. His piggy eyes widened in shock. Then he gave the chain a sharp jerk that felt like it would break my neck. Keats was still at the other end of the chain, getting dragged along in the scuffle.

"Give it up, Suit," he said. "You and this mangy mutt are compost. No point messing your pretty hair."

I knew any exertion would end my battle sooner. I also knew that four minutes without oxygen would fry my brain beyond further use. But that knowledge didn't stop me from fighting for my life, and for Keats' life. Another vision came into my head, replacing the image of the dumpster death. There was a farm, with green meadows and an alpaca. An alpaca... how strange. Keats was running like the wind, tail aloft. All this would be mine if only I could last a little longer.

I stopped trying to loosen the chain at my neck and grabbed it further down. Skint had shifted his focus momentarily to the skull and was trying to kick it into the darkness. That gave me the chance I needed. I yanked as hard as I could on the chain and pulled him off balance. The sudden slack sent me stumbling backwards, pulling Skint and Keats with me. Now we were out in the open space beyond the dumpster.

"Oh no you don't, Suit." His hands crawled back up the chain to tighten the loop. "I got too much to lose to let you win. That head you stole was in a gang once."

He bent over and the fingers of his free hand sank into my hair. He pulled my head up and then banged it hard on the asphalt. Stars popped behind my eyes and turned into fireworks when he did it again.

I flailed but eventually my hands fell away from the chain as my fingers numbed. He pulled up my head one more time to finish the job. Mist narrowed my field of vision, but I still saw a black and white blur jump onto his back. Keats seized Skint's ear, slipped off and hung there. The man yelled and released the chain. He stood up and spun around.

The dog didn't let go and his white paws flew out in a new and deadly pirouette.

I heard another scream, a familiar voice, and then all went black.

CHAPTER TEN

Jilly's green eyes were wide with worry when I opened mine and looked up at her. She was kneeling beside me, clutching my hand.

"My chest," I croaked. "Can't breathe." And then, "Where's Keats?"

She nodded in the direction of my chest. "The answer to both questions is right in front of you."

Groaning, I lifted my head to look. Keats was curled in a ball on my ribcage. His mismatched eyes met mine and then he leaned forward and licked my chin.

"He's okay? The heatstroke..."

"He's had water and seems totally fine. I'll take him to a vet to be sure."

I tried to lift my hand to pat him but the message didn't transmit from my brain to my fingertips. Jilly felt the twitch, however, and squeezed my hand again. "Just rest for a few minutes, okay? The paramedics will be back soon."

"Where's Skint?" A shudder ran from head to foot at the fragmented memory of what had just happened.

"Gone," she said, with a knowing look.

"Gone where?" I tried again to move and failed. "He's on the run?"

"He won't be running anytime soon. I arrived with the cops and we saw... well, Skint shook off the dog and was trying to—"

"Finish me off?"

"Yes. So they had to use their weapons."

"He's dead?" A mixture of horror and relief ran through me and suddenly my hands could move again.

She shook her head. "Not dead enough. But he won't be nearly as spry if he recovers. And the police assure me that the skull—and whatever else is under the sunflowers—will keep him out of the way indefinitely. He had a long record and they have reason to suspect there's more than one skull."

"Oh, good," I said.

"Good?" Something like a laugh slipped out.

"Not that there are multiple skulls. But that there's enough evidence to put him away if he survives." I managed to squeeze her hand back. "So, Keats is mine?"

"I already asked and the police said yes. I think they were a little surprised that was my top priority." She grinned. "I mean, after making sure you were okay, and that Skint was out of commission."

I closed my eyes for a second and took a deep breath. "What took you so darned long? It felt like forever."

"Traffic. It was totally gridlocked. I finally had to get out and run, and I managed to stop a cop and explain what was going on. I had already tried Jason, but he wasn't working tonight. Even the police had a heck of a time getting here." Tears filled her eyes and spilled over, dropping onto my face. "When I think about how just another two minutes could have..."

"It's okay. I'm okay."

She took a minute to gather herself and then forced a smile. "I wish you could have seen their faces when I told them you were running around with a skull in your purse."

"I felt terrible about leaving it in case it was some sweet old lady. But

Skint said it was a gang member." I shuddered again. "Not that anyone deserves to end up as fertilizer."

The paramedics and cops came over together. Soon I was on a stretcher covered in blankets. Keats struggled in Jilly's arms until they let him sit on my legs.

Jilly spoke to the police while the paramedics examined me and peered into my eyes. They asked me a series of questions, which I congratulated myself for getting right. Full marks for the dog hero.

"She's got a concussion," one paramedic announced. "We're taking her in for tests."

Jilly rushed to my side. "I should have known. You kept mumbling about a farm when you were coming to."

I nodded and winced. "I saw a beautiful farm. It was a dream, I guess. Or what heaven looks like. There was an alpaca."

The paramedic laughed. "No reason there can't be alpacas in heaven."

"In my heaven there is," I said. "And a border collie to herd them."

Jilly stood by while the police asked me a few questions. She corrected me gently in a few places, and I realized I might not be as sharp as I'd thought.

"Don't worry," she said. "It'll all come back." Glancing at the paramedics, she added, "Won't it?"

They both nodded, which gave me double reassurance. I looked at the cop. "Why would he keep a border collie in his yard instead of a real guard dog?"

The officer shrugged. "Easier to manage? Less conspicuous to neighbors? But I think he underestimated a border collie's intelligence."

Keats raised his head and directed his blue eye at the officer, as if to concur.

"We've got officers there now," he continued. "There's been a lot of rain recently and it washed out some of the soil. It wasn't hard to excavate."

"If the guy hadn't ignored the dog, he'd have seen that earlier," Jilly said. "So thank goodness for small mercies."

The cop said he'd be in touch soon and started to walk away.

"Wait," I said. "Can you cut the chain off him please?"

"I'll see what I can do," he said.

As the paramedics were about to lift me into the ambulance, we heard tires screeching and turned. A reporter came running over and aimed a camera in my face, firing questions at bewildering speed.

Keats sat up and stared at him, but Jilly did more than that. She moved between the stretcher and the reporter and then advanced. "My friend has a head injury. Please leave her alone to recover."

"We heard she killed someone to save the dog," he said. "She's a hero."

"She *is* a hero, but she didn't kill anyone. And nobody died."

"It's okay, Jilly," I said. "I don't mind telling them that Keats and I nearly bought the farm today. And that's what I'm going to do now: buy a farm."

Jilly stepped back to squeeze my arm. "Hush, Ivy."

"I saw it clearly when I passed out," I said.

"A near-death experience," the reporter said, zooming in. "You saw a farm?"

I nodded. "With an alpaca. A llama, too. And a couple of donkeys."

Jilly squeezed harder. "That's enough now, Ivy. You need to rest."

I smiled at the reporter. "She thinks I'm punch drunk. But I know what I saw."

"And you really risked your life for a dog?"

"Not just any dog. This is one gifted border collie." I touched Keats. "Can you show them your tricks?"

Keats jumped off the stretcher and did a beautiful pirouette on his hind legs. Then he walked backwards, still upright, before dropping to all fours and offering a white paw to the delighted reporter.

The cop had returned and cut the dog's collar with one snip. Keats was free at last.

"See?" I said, as he hopped back on the stretcher. "Some dogs are worth crawling around in a dumpster, smashing windows and getting strangled."

"So that's what smells," the reporter said.

"That dumpster was full of rats, too. It was so much worse than carrying the—"

Finally Jilly pinched me. Hard. "That's enough chitchat for now, my friend." Leaning over, she whispered. "You know how stories get blown out of proportion and spread on social media."

"I don't care," I said.

"You might later." She signalled the paramedics. "Let's roll, shall we?"

"How do you feel now?" the reporter called.

"Great." I tried to sit up as the paramedics pushed the stretcher to the ambulance. "Like I have a new leash on life." I rested my hand on Keats. "All because of this guy."

One of the paramedics pushed me back on the stretcher. "Down. Relax," he said. "You could have permanent brain damage."

I scratched Keats' ears. "We've got a second chance. Both of us. Who wouldn't want that?"

"Your chariot awaits," Jilly said, urging them to pick up the pace.

"Jilly, you've got to slow down and smell the sunflowers," I said.

"And you've got to seal those lips until your brains unscramble. You're babbling, and you never babble.

"Maybe I do now. New day, new Ivy."

"Hit it," Jilly called, sighing.

The ambulance doors closed and we drove off.

"Do you know what, Jilly?" I said, settling back with one hand resting between Keats' ears.

"What?" She took a rubber glove off the paramedic's tray and pulled it onto her right hand. Then she pulled up the blanket and started plucking garbage off my pant legs. There was a chicken wing, squashed fries and a variety of garnishes. Her lips parted so that she could breathe through her mouth to fend off my stench.

"I just beat the grim reaper," I said. "Now I've stared him in the face and I know for sure it's not me."

"Never was, my friend." She collected some hot peppers from the remains of my sock and dumped them into the plastic bag the paramedic gave her.

Keats nosed around the bag, hungry enough he'd eat week-old garbage.

"Don't even," Jilly said, moving the bag out of reach. "It's all high-end kibble for you from now on."

"She's right about that, buddy," I said. "Let's find greener pastures where we can live happily ever after."

"No more near-death experiences," Jilly said. "For either of you."

The paramedic offered me a little paper cup of water and I raised it. "I'll drink to that."

Keats gave his odd mumbling noises that sounded like agreement.

Jilly shook her head and pulled a soggy nacho chip off my shoe. "Why do I get the feeling this dog has brought more adventure into our lives than we can handle?"

I caught her arm with my free hand and squeezed. It felt good, safe and right to be sandwiched between my two best friends. "I get the same feeling about adventure ahead, Jilly. But together we can handle anything. You'll see."

Sign up for my mailing list at **ellenriggs.com/opt-in** to find out more about this series. My newsletter is full of funny stories and photos of my adorable dogs. You'll receive a free story, *The Cat and the Riddle*, which is EXCLUSIVE to subscribers. Don't miss out!

DOGCATCHER IN THE RYE

Dogcatcher In the Rye - Preview Chapter 1

Keats ran to the front window and stood on his hind legs to look out at the driveway. He didn't even lean on the wall, just stood upright like a circus dog. I'd taught him plenty of tricks, but that one he knew before we met a few months ago. He could turn a full circle in a few quick hops and never lost his balance. The slim, shaggy black-and-white dog with one blue eye and one brown was living proof of why border collies top the list on the canine intelligence scale.

"Who is it, buddy?" I asked. "Tell me it's not another casserole delivery."

He directed his blue eye at me, and I could have sworn it rolled. Keats had the most expressive face I'd ever seen on a dog. I was getting better at figuring out what he was thinking. And he was *always* thinking. Some days I was convinced he was smarter than me, if only because my brain hadn't fully recovered since the incident that had brought us together.

"Help me keep this short, okay?" I said, smoothing my hair. I wished I'd put on makeup earlier. When I lived in the city, there was no way I'd even think of opening the door without mascara, eyeliner and earrings. "Create a diversion if you need to. We've got a ton of errands in town."

Keats' tail wagged once, twice, then drifted down. It didn't look promising. With all the visitors we'd had since moving to the farm a week earlier, I'd barely been able to get anything done. The old tradition of stopping by with a warm welcome was alive and well in Clover Grove.

It was sweet, but time consuming. Keats had no patience for it at all. He was a dog who liked to be doing, not sitting around making small talk.

No one arrived empty handed. The cupboards that had been pretty much bare now held jam in five flavors and preserves both sweet and sour. The fridge and freezer were full of pies, cakes and heartier dishes. Mostly, there were eggs—dozens of them in shapes, sizes and colors I never knew existed. Meanwhile, there were about 40 generous hens in my own coop, producing more eggs than I could use, at least until my inn opened next month. Hopefully my guests would love omelets.

When I left Clover Grove for college 15 years ago, the town had been moving away from its agricultural roots. The homesteading trend was bringing people back to the land in droves. I had mocked that trend once, but now I was basically doing the same. Things had a way of biting you in the butt in farm country.

I opened the door at the precise moment someone gave a firm knock. It startled me and maybe that's why I gasped even before I saw Lloyd Boyce standing on the porch in a uniform. I hadn't seen Lloyd since high school, and I hoped time had been kinder to me than it had been to him. His ginger hair had not so much silvered as faded to a dull tan and his freckled face was lined and haggard. Still, his eyes were a striking blue and he held himself as if he knew how to use his charm if he felt like it.

"Well, hello Lloyd," I said. "How nice to see you. You haven't changed a bit."

It was the kind of polite lie you learned to tell early in Clover Grove and I'd never outgrown the habit. My former colleagues had teased me about it, but it hadn't slowed my climb up the corporate ranks.

"Hi Ivy," Lloyd said. "You look great, too."

I could tell from the slight twitch of his lips that he probably meant it. In high school, he'd run in the same circles as Asher, my older brother. Lloyd had always given me the creeps but I must have hidden it well because he invited me to his senior prom. Ash was outraged—the invitation defied "bro code"—but I'd declined anyway. My tenth grade social life wasn't exactly thriving but there was no way I was dating Lloyd Boyce.

Maybe Lloyd remembered that old rejection, too, because his eyes dropped to his black work boots, which looked freshly polished. His black uniform with the town crest was crisp and fit well. The belt around his waist had a holster over his left hip that held what appeared to be a can of pepper spray. A short baton balanced that out on his right hip, and another device hung further back. The weapons made me even more uneasy.

"What can I do for you, today, Lloyd? I don't see a pie or preserves, so I'm assuming it's not a housewarming visit."

"Right. I'm here on business." Lloyd pressed his thin lips together and peered over my shoulder. "There's been a complaint."

"A complaint? Already? I've only been here a week. I haven't had time to get into trouble." I had a good poker face after more than a decade of work in human resources and I was grateful for it now. "I mean, other than eating too much pie. Could I interest you in a slice? I've got apple, blueberry and pecan. You really can't go wrong with any of them."

"I don't eat pie on duty," Lloyd said, rising on the toes of his boots to look over my other shoulder.

"Let me get you a glass of water then. Or a cup of coffee." I scanned the gravel driveway, expecting to see cars arriving with nosy neighbors. It wouldn't be long till the Clover Grove rumor mill started churning about Lloyd's visit. If it wasn't already.

His eyes came back to land on me. "Where is he?"

"Where is who? I'm on my own here till my first paying guests arrive."

That caught his attention. "Guests?"

"Clients. Customers. Maybe you've heard that I'm opening a small inn. Coming from Boston, I know how eager people are to enjoy the farm experience."

"This isn't a farm." He shook his head in apparent disgust. "It's a petting zoo."

"Hobby farm, then. Would you like to come down to the barn and meet the alpaca? It's a beautiful day for a stroll."

September was my favorite month in Clover Grove. The worst of the heat had lifted, but it was still balmy. My goal was to open before the fall colors came in. The surrounding hills had some of the best views in the country.

"I get enough walking in my job," Lloyd said. "And I don't have any interest in your misfits."

"Misfits! That's a terrible thing to say. The rescued animals here are all very sweet." Except for the pig, who was intent on killing me, but no need to mention that. As an Animal Services field agent, Lloyd might take issue.

"The County doesn't endorse this farm, Ivy. I hope you know that. It's been nothing but trouble, especially after that heiress took over and started her stupid online show. It attracted swarms of idiots."

"I have full confidence that the County will enjoy the tourist dollars my guests bring. I think my inn's going to be a big hit. People will love frolicking with the goats, milking the cows and seeing lambs being born. They'll eat five-star meals and go home feeling restored."

"Sounds like a commercial," he said, taking a step back.

I pressed my lips together to stop more words from tumbling out. My nerves were showing. Initially, I'd been on the fence about coming home to Clover Grove, but the former owner, Hannah Pemberton, had tracked me down in Boston and asked me to buy Runaway Farm. *Insisted*, actually. It was the strangest thing I'd ever experienced, other than the incident that prompted the offer—an incident I was desperate to forget. I couldn't help but think the universe was pulling me home. Now that I was back here, I had moments of wishing the universe had sent me someplace else. When forces like that align, however, who are we to argue?

"What happened with Hannah isn't my business," I said. The

online show he despised, The Princess and the Pig, was hilarious and provocative. I was watching old episodes to educate myself about Runaway Farm and its makeover into an inn. "But I assure you I'm serious about this inn and the community. I have to be."

Lloyd shook his head and frowned. "City slickers."

I wasn't sure whether he was insulting me or my future guests, so I let it slide. "Eventually all chickens come home to roost, I guess."

His eyes lit up and I mentally cursed myself for giving him the opening he wanted.

"Speaking of chickens," he said. "Edna Evans called Animal Services today saying your dog attacked her hens."

Keats chose that exact moment to stick his head between my knees and stare up at Lloyd. Then he gave a sharp woof. The dog had told me off often enough that I knew it was a reproof.

"Those chickens were on my property," I said. "Keats simply rounded them up and took them home. Not a single feather was ruffled."

"Edna said they came rushing onto her porch clucking like the devil himself was after them."

Keats *had* been a trifle overeager. He had more experience herding sheep and the hens' vertical moves added complexity to the maneuver. Still, all the hens had arrived safely.

"That's quite an exaggeration, Lloyd. Keats is a herding dog. I've been working with him for months."

"Herding? In the city?" He gave me a skeptical look.

"All over the state, actually. Would you like to see his certificates? He's a prizewinner."

Keats gave a high-pitched whine, as if my bragging were beneath him. It was beneath both of us, since we'd only passed beginner level. He was a natural, but we were just getting started.

Lloyd shook his head. "Doesn't matter. Your dog was chasing livestock and that's not tolerated here. The consequences start with a fine and end with—"

I tensed, squeezing my shins together. Keats made a strangled sound and pulled back. "I hope you're not threatening my dog, Lloyd. Keats is the best dog on earth. I moved back here to give him a better life."

"You moved back because some heiress gave you a sweet deal on this place. How'd you manage that, anyway?"

I glanced around, feeling almost embarrassed at my good fortune. The big old red brick farmhouse had been renovated beautifully, keeping the best features of the original and adding luxurious finishes. There was a new wing at the back with spacious bedrooms and spa-like bathrooms for the guests. I still felt like I was living in a boutique hotel, but it would become home soon enough. My sister, Daisy, was helping me add the final touches.

"Just lucky, I guess," I said. "Hannah saw an article about me saving Keats from a dangerous criminal, and thought I needed a break."

"I save dogs every day and no one gives me breaks like that."

His face twitched into a frown and for a second I felt sorry for him. "You've done well for yourself, Lloyd, at least from what Ash tells me."

"What'd your brother say?" Now he sounded worried.

I bit my lower lip. Asher was an officer with Wolff County's police department. Sometimes he shared confidential things because I was out of town and couldn't get him in trouble with gossip. Now that I lived here, I'd have to be more careful, especially since my memory wasn't always my friend these days.

"Something about a girl...?" I began. "You got married?"

"I got divorced," he said. "Well, almost."

"Oh. I'm sorry, Lloyd. That must have been hard."

He waved away my pity. "I've found someone new. You probably remember Mandy McCain."

"The baker, of course. Her grandmother runs Clover Grove Country Store. I've loved that place forever."

"The store's outdated now, but the land's worth a bomb with the way the town's developing. Mandy should sell while she can and get out." His frown lines deepened. "This place isn't what you remember, Ivy."

"I bet Clover Grove still has a big heart, just like when we were growing up."

He gave a little smirk as he pulled a device from his equipment belt. "I'll show some heart today by letting you off with the minimum fine. As a homecoming present."

I gasped. "A fine! Lloyd, you can't fine me for escorting someone's hens from my property to their own home. That's ridiculous."

"You're not in Boston anymore, Ivy. We take animal welfare seriously here."

Heat whooshed up from my belly and blew out my diplomacy circuits. "You're a dogcatcher. You round up strays so the County can euthanize them. How is that taking animal welfare seriously?"

Color rose under Lloyd's tan, swamping his freckles. "I'm just following the rules. Your dog was chasing livestock. End of story."

"Oh, it's not the end of this story. I'm going to contest this fine. What are my rights?"

Lloyd shrugged. "You have the right to pay the fine now or pay double if you're late."

Keats whined, as if to warn me, and I took a deep breath. I didn't lose my temper often, but when I did... well, the last time landed me on the news, in the hospital, and ultimately out of a job. Losing it again now certainly wouldn't help my farm-themed inn. I didn't want a blot on my record with Animal Services.

Maybe it wasn't too late to turn things around. I took another deep breath and closed my eyes. Normally my best friend, Jilly Blackwood, would step in when I lost my tact, but she wouldn't be here to visit for another few weeks. I'd just have to channel my inner executive—the one who'd hired and fired hundreds of people for a large corporation.

"Lloyd, I'm sorry about my tone. I'm just so anxious about all of this." I gestured from the big red barn to the paddock, where two Holstein heifers leaned over the fence watching us. "There's so much riding on the launch of my inn. Obviously I don't want to get off on the wrong foot with Animal Services."

Lloyd didn't even look up from his device. His big fingers moved with surprising speed, until he punched a button with his thumb. A bright orange ticket spit out the bottom, like a neon tongue. The whirring noise it made covered the sound of Keats's low grumble... or so I hoped. I snapped my fingers and the dog subsided.

"I heard that." Lloyd tore off the ticket with a flourish. "He growled."

"He did not growl. He makes mumbling sounds all the time. That's all."

"I'm in animal control. I know an aggressive dog when I hear it."

"Aggressive! Are you kidding me? He's a border collie. He herds sheep and does agility. He dances on his hind legs while balancing a peanut on his nose." I moved aside to reveal my sweet dog. "Sit pretty, Keats."

Keeping his butt firmly planted, Keats sat upright, his white front paws dangling. His blue eye looked a bit eerie as he stared up at Lloyd. Maybe the dogcatcher thought so too, because he took another step back.

"Just keep your dog away from livestock, Ivy," he said, holding out the ticket.

I refused to take it and it flapped in the breeze. From the paddock, one of the cows let out a long, low moo.

"You're making everyone sad, Lloyd," I said. "Won't you please reconsider?"

"The ticket's already on record. No going back," he said. "Take it, or I'll drop it by the post office and word will get around faster. Your call."

"The word's already gotten around, I'm sure. Everyone knows your truck. You're putting a black mark on my inn before I've even opened."

Walking down the stairs, his shoulders shifted in a shrug. "I have the feeling we'll meet again before long, Ivy. You take care, now."

I stepped back inside, slammed the screen door, and then slammed the wooden door for good measure. Outside the boots clomped back up the stairs and I heard the lid of the old metal mailbox creak open and shut. He had probably dumped that ticket inside.

The heavy footsteps moved away and I flipped the bird at the door. The clomping stopped, almost as if Lloyd could sense it. Finally he moved off, and then his tires crunched over the gravel as he pulled away.

Stooping, I gathered Keats into a hug. He didn't love being squeezed but endured it for me. "The fun's just beginning, buddy. Get ready for a bumpy ride."

Dogcatcher In the Rye - Preview Chapter 2

I almost enjoyed the 10-minute drive to the Clover Grove Country Store that afternoon. It was sunny and warm, and the smell of green meadows and manure drifted in from the passenger window as Keats stuck his head out and surveyed his new domain. The dog had clearly put his past behind him, and I needed to do that, too.

Our ride was far from smooth, however, because the big black pickup truck that came with the farm had a standard transmission. My older sister Daisy had taught me to drive on a stick when I was 16 but it wasn't as much like riding a bike as I'd hoped. Sometimes the truck lurched and stalled out—always in embarrassing places, like a four-way stop where people could see me. No doubt it cemented their view that the city slicker should have stayed in her high-rise. But every drive got a little bit better and I liked riding above the crowd. Or as much above the crowd as you could be in an area where everyone seemed to drive trucks.

From the outside, Myrtle's Store—as the Clover Grove Country Store was more commonly known—looked like it hadn't changed a bit since I came with my brother and sisters for penny candy long ago. The big green sign with its ornate gold lettering had a quaint charm, and the fresh white paint made it look well cared for. It *was* well cared for by Myrtle McCain, who'd been running the store for nearly 50 years, after taking over from her dad, and his dad before him. The store was older than Wolff County itself and was something people could rely on in a changing landscape.

Inside, Myrtle's Store was a curious mix of the old and the new. Some of the shelves held dusty old hardware supplies and fishing gear that may have predated my existence. Behind the cash register, however, hung cell phones, and electric razors and toothbrushes. There was a clear plastic shield over the counter that covered rows of lottery tickets and calling cards. The penny candy had been replaced by racks of chocolate bars, some imported from Europe. Myrtle would order in almost anything you wanted, which is why there was such a haphazard array of products in the grocery aisles.

A couple of years ago, she'd installed a long laminate bar along the wide front window. The stools were rarely empty. Clover Grove residents hoisted themselves up to watch the local traffic and enjoy a good cup of coffee. The makeshift café was meant as a showcase for Myrtle's granddaughter, Mandy, who was a gifted baker. They rotated through a long list of tasty treats. If you really wanted a lemon square, you came before noon on Tuesday, because they were gone by two p.m.

Myrtle's silver head was bent over a laptop when I walked in with Keats. "Ivy," she said, looking up with twinkling blue eyes and a welcoming smile. "You look wonderful."

That was about as true as what I'd said earlier to Lloyd. My hair was in a ponytail and I hadn't bothered to doll up for errands. I probably looked as frazzled as I felt.

"Thanks, Myrtle. You look well, too." In fact, she looked far younger than the 75 years she claimed. Some said she was closer to 80.

"Couldn't be better." She got up and leaned over the counter. "But I'm a bit worried about *you* and your handsome sidekick."

I expected this but my face flushed anyway. "You've heard. Honestly, I forgot how fast news travels in Clover Grove and all of Wolff County." The name came out as "Woof," like it did with anyone born and bred here. Pronouncing the "L" instantly showed you were an outsider.

"Oh, honey, don't you worry about Lloyd Boyce. He's a fool, but his bark is worse than his bite."

Lloyd and his colleagues in Animal Services were widely reviled in this pet-loving county. It hadn't always been that way, but the meteoric rise of a city to our west called Dorset Hills—known for being the best city for dog-lovers—had put pressure on Wolff County. Land prices had gone up because people wanted to buy close to the bigger center. Plus, draconian policies about dog behavior in the neighboring city had led to an increase in "problem dogs" being dumped in Wolff County. Our Animal Services had grown as a result, and their staff were trying to grapple with the effects of being in the shadow of a quirky tourist attraction.

"Edna Evans reported Keats for chasing her chickens," I said. "All he did was herd them off my property and safely onto hers."

"Gotta love the border collie drive," Myrtle said. She peered over the counter at Keats and his mouth opened in a sloppy grin of agreement. "Always had one myself until a few years ago. Can't keep up anymore."

I nodded. "This one hardly ever closes his eyes."

Since I'd rescued Keats as a malnourished adolescent, he'd put on nearly 20 pounds and his coat was now thick and shiny. Now just over a year old, his energy seemed boundless.

"And beautiful eyes they are," she said. Keats waved his tail, complete with white plume, to signify his approval of Myrtle. He didn't take to everyone, but she'd made the grade. Looking up from the dog, she reached for the list in my hand. "What can I get the innkeeper today?"

"Strike off whatever you can," I said. "I'll get the rest in town."

Myrtle cocked her head as she read. "Curtain rods... I think there's a few in the stock room. Definitely have a stainless steel Dutch oven back there, and yes to the portable vacuum. Not sure about the air pump, though." She looked up. "This could take a bit. Why don't you have a coffee?"

"Sure. What's the treat of the day?"

"Apple cheesecake's the Monday special. A personal favorite."

"Done." I headed over to the bar. Two of the five stools were already taken, and I chose the one on the end. "Morning," I said to the couple down the row. They were probably in their late sixties, with gray hair and matching, oversized glasses. After a quick nod, they went right back to doing the newspaper crossword puzzle.

Mandy came over with my coffee and a slab of cheesecake. She was slender and pale, with dirty blonde hair and brilliant blue eyes like her grandmother's. "Hey Ivy, you're going to like this one," she said.

"Everything you bake is an automatic yes for me, Mandy," I said. "I'll put on 10 pounds before the inn even opens."

She gave me a shy smile. Back in school, Mandy rarely spoke, but discovering her baking genius had given her confidence.

I took a bite, chewed and then closed my eyes in bliss.

"Should we put it on the list?" she asked.

"Heck yeah," I said. "My guests are going to keep coming back for this alone."

"Have you lined up any customers yet?"

"Not yet, but I won't start putting the word out till everything's just right. Daisy says I'm a control freak, and she's not far wrong." I took a sip of coffee, staring at Mandy over the brim. "Your boyfriend gave me a ticket this morning." I nudged Keats with my foot. "More specifically, he gave Keats a ticket."

Color rushed up Mandy's throat and into her cheeks. "Lloyd isn't my boyfriend."

"Really? He said you were seeing each other."

"We've chatted a few times when our bowling leagues met up in Brenton, that's all." She leaned in so the crossword couple couldn't hear. "His divorce isn't even final."

"Okay, well that's a relief. I was worried you'd take his advice to sell the store and leave town. You know I'm counting on your baking to help build my name."

"Sell the store? Of course not." She turned to the counter but

Myrtle was nowhere in sight. "I promise to keep Runaway Farm in baked goods for many years to come."

As soon as Mandy walked away, the older couple looked up from their crossword. They both had plump, kind faces. The woman pointed at Keats with her pencil. "Is this the dog Lloyd Boyce targeted this morning?"

I nodded. "Unauthorized herding of a neighbor's chickens."

I expected her to laugh but her eyes filled with tears. "Lloyd killed my dog, you know. Sweetest shepherd cross you could ever meet."

Her husband patted her shoulder. "Don't get yourself upset, now, honey. It's been years."

"Feels like yesterday." The woman swallowed hard. "I'm Margie Hodgson and this is my husband, Fred. I left our dog Gunner tied up outside the butcher shop and someone reported that he snapped at a child who poked him with a stick. There was absolutely no evidence but Lloyd Boyce rolled up in his van, snagged Gunner in a noose and dragged him away." She lifted her heavy glasses and swiped at the tears with her sleeve. "I will never forget that heartrending howl as long as I live. And I will never forgive that man."

"Margie." Fred Hodgson squeezed her hand to get her attention. "What's a five-letter word for Batman's nemesis?"

"Joker," Margie said. "Idiot. Loser. Lloyd."

"Sounds about right." The voice came from behind and I spun on my stool to see a tall woman with dark eyes and immaculately flat-ironed brown hair. Her jacket was high end, although it probably had some years on it. "That's my ex-husband you're talking about."

"I'm sorry," I said quickly. "I had an unfortunate encounter with Lloyd this morning."

"I had an unfortunate eight years with Lloyd." Her laugh had a bitter edge. "I'm Nadine Boyce, soon to be Tanner again. You must be Ivy Galloway. I heard about what happened."

I stood, careful not to step on Keats, and shook her hand. "Sounds like everyone has."

"I helped your sister Daisy buy her house," Nadine said, seamlessly slipping a business card into my hand. "If Lloyd drives you out, give me a call."

"Lloyd will never drive me out of Runaway Farm, but thanks."

Nadine smiled over her shoulder as she walked into the grocery aisle. "I hope not, but you wouldn't be the first. Keep a close eye on that handsome dog of yours."

When I looked back, the Hodgsons had slipped away. Maybe they didn't want to be anywhere near Lloyd's ex. I glanced out the window in time to see them wave from the parking lot and raised my hand in return.

"Myrtle!" A man stood at the counter and bellowed. "Hello! Myrtle!"

She hurried out of the back room, flushed from the effort of digging up the items on my list. Running a place like this had to be hard on a woman of her age.

"Why hello, Brian. You look wonderful today."

Okay, now I *knew* it was a polite lie because Brian looked way less wonderful than I did. He was probably only a few years older than me, yet his beard was graying. His hair was thinning and he'd tied what was left in a scraggly ponytail. That was never a good look on a man, in my opinion.

He grunted at Myrtle. "Did my package come?"

She shook her head. "I told you I'd call you the second it did. Don't I always keep my word?"

His shoulders slumped. "No. You didn't bring in the Vegemite like you promised."

Myrtle laughed. "It's coming. Hold onto your kangaroos."

He smiled and the mood lightened instantly. "Call me," he reminded her, turning to go. "Don't leave that package unattended for one second, okay? It's valuable."

"Promise repeated," Myrtle said. As he turned, she glanced over at me and rolled her eyes.

Brian had to step around a tall, heavy-set man on his way out. The guy was hard to miss, with his shaved head and tattoos creeping over his collar. Even from my spot at the window, I could see a bright yellow serpent twisting up and around the man's ear. There was a hint of red where the tongue darted out that made me shudder. When I worked in HR, I'd struggled to put my bias against tattoos aside in hiring. They were so common now, but to me, tattoos locked people down as who they had been, rather than who they could become.

"I'll take a cup of tea," he told Myrtle. His voice was low but surprisingly pleasant. "And the treat of the day, whatever it is."

Myrtle nodded. "Coming up, Graham. You staying?"

"On the run," he said. "Gotta get the shop open and make a few people scream."

She laughed. "One day I'll get you to tattoo a little sheepdog on my shoulder. What do you think?"

"Sure. For you, there are painkillers."

His grin was unexpectedly warm, but the minute he turned to go it faded and all I could focus on was the snake again. Until I noticed the blue scorpion on his eyebrow.

I was anxious to get going but Myrtle was still juggling a stream of customers. One rather elegant older man in a nice sports jacket came in for a package of cigars. She handed them to him with the usual smile, and said, "Here you go, Arthur. Staying for coffee today?"

Arthur glanced in my direction and his eyes dropped to Keats. "Not if you're letting dogs in here, now. Isn't that against bylaws for a restaurant?"

"It's not a restaurant," Myrtle said smoothly.

I swivelled on my stool to face him squarely and said, "This is a service animal."

Arthur raised one salt-and-pepper eyebrow. "You don't say."

His tone raised my hackles, and that in turn raised Keats'. I didn't have to look down to know because it had happened before. The dog seemed to know what I felt almost before I did.

"I do say." I smiled to take the edge off the comment. "This dog is best in class."

It was true that Keats was best in class in beginner herding, but our therapy dog classes had been less notable. He had his own notions about how to provide emotional support and mostly that meant keeping me too busy to think. It was a valid plan and worked for the most part.

Arthur gave a little smirk. "Well, I'm not sharing counter space with a dog showing its fangs."

"He is not!" I didn't dare look at Keats. I was 100 percent sure his fangs weren't showing and I wouldn't give this guy the pleasure of showing doubt.

"Fine, I just don't want dog hair in my cheesecake." He accepted the container Myrtle handed him. "You and Fido have a good day, now."

I glared after him as he slid behind the wheel of his Mercedes.

"Never mind Arthur," Nadine Boyce said, coming back and perching on the stool beside me. The grocery basket she set on the floor at her feet held a quart of milk, cheese, tinned chickpeas and what looked like a box of rat poison. "His bark is worse than his bite."

"That's what people say about Lloyd," I told her.

"Well, *that's* a polite lie," Nadine said, smiling. "Lloyd's bite will leave you festering and in need of amputation. At least that's how I'm handling it."

I couldn't help smiling back. "I know divorce is never easy, especially in a small town."

Nadine nodded, shifting to let Myrtle collect the newspapers the Hodgsons had left in their hurry to go. "You've really got to think things through before you make the cut. It can get ugly fast."

I looked over my shoulder, wondering if she knew Lloyd had lined up her replacement already. Mandy had disappeared into the back room, possibly embarrassed to have so many people dissing Lloyd. But if she wanted to date the dogcatcher, she was going to need thicker skin.

"It sounds like your business is thriving," I said, to change the subject. "I absolutely love Daisy's house and she couldn't be happier."

Nadine beamed. "That is so nice to hear. Say hi to her for me."

"Will do." I slid off the stool. "We're meeting later to choose curtains for the inn." I picked up Keats' leash and he danced at the end of it, relieved to get moving.

"You've got my card?" she said.

I patted my bag. "But really, there's no way I'd ever sell Runaway Farm."

"That's what the last owner said." Her eyes crinkled. "Some say it's cursed, but I don't believe in that kind of thing."

A shiver ran down my spine and Keats pressed closer, whining almost inaudibly.

"Then I'd better pick up some sage and burn it tonight," I said, heading for the cash register. "Daisy said it'll flush out anything but your septic system."

Dogcatcher In the Rye - Preview Chapter 3

"Do not let Nadine Boyce scare you," my sister said, towing me around the biggest department store in Clover Grove. In fact, it was the only legit department store, and its selection was eclectic and dated. Luckily, Daisy had a way of seeing something unique and stylish in what looked dull and boring to me.

"I won't," I said, trailing after her. Of all the tasks involved in getting an inn up and running, interior design was the one I hated most. I wasn't fazed at all by mucking out stalls when Charlie, my farm manager, was off duty. But take me to a department store and my throat practically seized. I was suffocating.

"Is that you panting, or Keats?" Daisy asked, keeping her eyes on the drapery panels hanging on tall racks.

"Both. We don't like being trapped inside." I paced back and forth, and Keats followed, staring up at me with his brown eye—the sympathetic one. "Do we, buddy?"

Keats offered his mumbled agreement. He always had plenty to say, even if I didn't understand all of it.

"You worked in a corporate cubicle for ten years, Ivy," Daisy said. She gave me a look without even turning her head. I didn't need to see it to know it was there. My older sister had been giving me the same look of incredulous disgust for the 33 years I was on the planet. She was the eldest in our family of six kids, and the first recipient of Mom's flora-themed names. After her came Lily, Poppy and Violet, golden boy Asher, and finally me. Mom's name was Dahlia, and she was about as subtle as the showiest variety.

"I've escaped all that now," I said. "Remember the year I criss-crossed the country firing people? My boss called me the grim reaper."

"You paid your dues and collected your bonus." She carried two curtain panels over to a window to inspect them in natural light. "Nothing to be ashamed of."

Daisy was always practical. I guess she had to be, looking after us while Mom worked overtime in a series of low-paying jobs. My sister's hair was even darker than mine, but already more salt than pepper. We'd probably aged her prematurely, and then her own kids—two sets of twin boys—finished the job.

"I'm not ashamed. Just happy to be out of there." I stared at the fabric she waved under my nose. "Daisy, they all look the same to me."

This time her look of disgust hit me head on. "The same! One is silver and one is pewter."

"It's two shades of gray." I grinned sheepishly. "Maybe my vision was affected in the accident."

My sister pinned me with hazel eyes that were also a little darker than mine. "That wasn't an accident. It was a violent attack that almost killed you."

I tried to hold in the shudder. Daisy was the only one who spoke plainly in our family. Sometimes it seemed like she was the only one who spoke plainly in all of Clover Grove. I valued her honesty, but more so when it was directed at someone else. Especially Asher.

"It didn't kill me. And no matter what the cost, it was worth it to save Keats."

Her eyes turned into sharp points. "I know you adore this dog, but rescuing him single-handedly from a felon wasn't your smartest move."

"I wasn't alone. I had Jilly," I said. "And I don't regret it one bit."

"Ivy. That guy almost bashed your brains in, and you haven't recovered fully yet. It's not something to be cavalier about."

My fingers went to a lump hidden under my hair that was probably permanent now. "I'm not being cavalier. I just want to put all that behind me. And the attack, if that's what you want to call it, brought me the farm, too, remember. So it all worked out, right?"

She continued to stare at me for a moment and then her eyes dropped to the fabric again. "You've changed, Ivy."

"Isn't change inevitable?"

"Here's the thing," she said, walking back to the racks and shoving panels aside. "You've got to set a mood with your inn. People need to come through the door and have an instant emotion. Pewter will bring awe. Is awe the emotion you want?"

I knelt beside Keats and shook my head. "Nope. Not awe."

"What then?"

"I want them to feel relief that they've escaped the pressures of the real world, if only for a weekend. I want them to feel comfortable and safe, and ultimately tranquil."

There was silence above me, and I looked up to find Daisy staring at me with an expression I hadn't seen before.

"That's more like it," she said, crooking her fingers to make me stand. "How does this one make you feel?" She held out a different gray panel and traced the silver pattern etched into it. "What's this?"

"I don't know... an amoeba?"

Again she pulled the panel down and led me to the window. "Look closer."

I stared at the velvety fabric and tried to focus. "Is it... a pig?"

"Yes," she said, grinning. "Silver pigs."

I laughed out loud. "That's perfect! A mix of elegance and country kitsch. You're a genius."

She laughed, too, shrugging off the praise. "The truth is always right before your eyes. You just have to look hard enough."

Carrying the panel to the department cashier, she asked for a dozen sets of curtains.

"All the same?" I asked.

"KISS principle." She checked her phone and shook her head. "I always tell the boys to 'keep it simple, stupid,' and they mostly do."

I kept my mouth shut out of gratitude. Daisy's boys were sweet hooligans who spent most of their time wrestling, running or rummaging for food.

After we'd finished, she studied me in silence while we crossed the parking lot. I pretended not to notice.

"I'm not buying it, Ivy Rose Galloway," she said at last. All the girls in our family shared the same middle name, because Mom had run out of good floral options.

"Buying what?"

"This easygoing act. You've always had the worst temper in the entire family."

I laughed as I unlocked my truck. "Wouldn't you have a temper if you came last—after the golden boy Mom always wanted and before she got dumped by Dad? Anyway, that's ancient history. Do you think I'd have been successful in HR if I'd had a bad temper?"

"You drove it underground but it still pops up. Like this morning. I heard you got snippy with Lloyd Boyce."

I knew she'd find out but I'd expected a little more time. Daisy lived on the other side of Clover Grove, a half-hour drive from Runaway Farm. "Good news sure travels fast."

"Edna Evans called Nora Peters and she emailed Mom, who asked me to handle it."

I sighed. Three decades later, Mom was still delegating family management to Daisy. It wasn't fair; my sister had her hands full raising the boys and working three part-time jobs. Her real passion was interior design, and I wanted to help her get launched.

"What is there to handle? I got a ticket from Animal Services. I'll pay it and make sure it's the last one."

"You will *not* pay that ticket," she said, piling curtains into the back seat of the truck. "The County could bring it up anytime and prevent you from expanding or renovating. You know this farm's been a political sore spot. That's why the previous owner got rid of it."

"That's not true. Hannah weathered out the politics when the land transferred to Wolff County. Clover Grove has no issue with livestock."

"Not the typical farm animals, but someone's bound to raise a concern about the alpaca and llamas at some point. And that someone is Lloyd Boyce."

She spit out the name like it tasted sour. Like many people, she'd had run-ins with him over her series of rescue dogs.

I pulled the tie out of my ponytail and raked my fingers through my hair. "How about we cross that bridge when we come to it, Daisy?"

"You got a great deal on Runaway Farm, but you're pouring your life savings into it, too. You can't afford to have Lloyd ruin this."

"My inn will bring new business into Clover Grove. The County should be grateful."

Leaning against the truck, she folded her arms. "Clover Grove isn't like you remembered."

"I can see that. Now it's pies and jam and fresh egg deliveries. When did that all start?"

It was Daisy's turn to shudder. "I don't even know when the tide turned to homesteading. One day I realized someone had stolen our normal small town and replaced it with this sweet little village. And it is sweet, but there's a current of something else underneath."

"What else?" I felt a breeze on the back of my neck that made me hug myself, although it was a warm day. Looking down, I saw Keats' ruff was standing on end, and his ears pricked up.

Daisy just shrugged. "I can't explain it. You'll see for yourself soon enough."

I gave a nervous laugh. "Is this where you get woo-woo and tell me to smudge the house with sage?"

For the first time all day, she truly smiled. Daisy was the prettiest of all the girls in our family, and the rest of us weren't bad, either. "That's a good idea. Let's smudge the farm tomorrow when I'm over to measure for rugs. But you can't smudge an entire town, Ivy."

"Why not? We could take the truck for a joyride tonight and smudge Woof County."

She laughed out loud. "People would talk, and I wouldn't blame them."

"They always talked about us, and I guess they always will." I opened the front door and gestured for Keats to jump through to the passenger seat. The truck was tall but border collies came wired with springs. "I'm not going to be a slave to gossip anymore."

Settling her sunglasses on her nose, Daisy said, "Then you'd better stop annoying your neighbors. Edna's the queen of gossip and she's right next door to you."

"Message received. I know what I have to do."

She let her glasses slide down and stared at me. "You do."

It was a statement, not a question. As if I hadn't learned a single thing since she walked me to kindergarten.

"Yeah, I do. I'll take some jam and a few dozen eggs over there and suck up to Edna Evans. Pronto."

The glasses stayed on the bridge of her nose, telling me I'd missed the mark. "Like smudging, sucking up is never a bad idea. But that's not what I meant and you know it."

"Daisy, Lloyd said there was no way around paying this ticket. If you've got a better idea than jam and eggs, just tell me."

She gave me the "duh" look reserved for special occasions of sibling idiocy. "Let Asher take care of it. Obviously."

"I am not asking my cop brother to make my Animal Services fine disappear."

"Why not? He's helped me out in a pinch and I know he'd help you."

Now I stared at *her* over my shades. "What kind of pinch?"

She sighed. "There was an incident with the boys and graffiti, down at Hoggs Bridge."

"That's all?"

There was a long pause. "The younger boys had light fingers. That's all I'm saying."

"Huh." I was surprised. Daisy ruled with an iron fist and the older boys were now fine young men.

"You can 'huh' all you like, but you have no idea how hard it's been with Reese and Beaton." She pushed her long bangs out of her eyes and sighed. "They're challenging."

I squeezed her arm. "It's okay. I can run this problem by Asher."

"You do that." She started backing away, toward her battered gray minivan. "Heading home now?"

"Nope. Few errands to run, and then I'm heading into the hills to let Keats stretch his legs."

Keats let out a little yip of excitement and Daisy said, "Don't tell me that dog understands English."

I slipped behind the wheel and scratched his chest. "Not yet but give him time."

She rolled her eyes. "Make sure you spread those curtains flat when you get home so they don't wrinkle, okay?"

"Got it." I turned the key in the ignition. "No wrinkles at Runaway Inn. Except the ones I'm getting."

"Oh, and Ivy?" Daisy said. "We treat dogs like dogs around here. Don't be that weird lady people talk about."

"I spent ten years as a paragon," I said, grinning as I put the truck in gear. "It's time to let my hair down."

WHEN WE GOT BACK from town that evening, Keats and I took a walk around the property. We'd made it to the trails above town earlier, but a chatty woman with a yappy Yorkshire terrier called Sparkles had slowed us down. As a soon-to-be innkeeper, I felt I had to be friendly with everyone.

Runaway Farm sat on about 20 acres now, and it was far deeper than it was wide. Past owners had sold much of the land, but what was left was lovely. There was a well-worn trail that wound around gentle hills and through wooded areas of deciduous and cedar trees. There were four orchards, from ancient to middle-aged. The apples from the youngest were apparently quite tasty.

The sun was already low when we started out but there was plenty of light to see the path, and I always felt safe with Keats. He ranged out ahead and circled back to check on me again and again. This dog didn't miss much, and while he was always "on" he wasn't frenetic. At least as long as he got a good run every day, which was a pleasure for both of us after city life.

So when Keats ran out and stayed out, I paid attention. Then he started barking in a way I'd never heard before. I didn't like the sound of it and stopped in my tracks. There were coyotes around, and wild boars, too. Something sure had Keats rattled, and when I called, he only came halfway back, his white tuxedo chest shining in the setting sun. Turning, he raced back the way he'd come.

If it were a predator, surely Keats wouldn't lead me into its jaws. There must be something he wanted to me to see.

"What is it, Keats?" I called, trying to sound big and menacing. I made a mental note to bring pepper spray and my sheep hook on my evening strolls. A reformed city girl couldn't be too careful.

Coming over the last small hill, I found Keats running back and forth at the edge of a field that had grown wild since previous owners had stopped farming the land. It was still tall after a nice summer.

My steps slowed until I got close enough to see what Keats was fussing about. Something dark was sticking out of the rye field.

When I got close enough, I bent over a pair of big black boots. The heels had sunk into the damp soil, and scuffed toes pointed to the sunset sky. Manure and hay was caked in the treads.

And unless I was much mistaken, the boots were still attached to the uniformed legs of Lloyd Boyce.

Join Ivy and Keats as they sleuth their way through Clover Grove in the next book, *Dogcatcher in the Rye*.

More Books by Ellen Riggs

Bought-the-Farm Cozy Mystery Series

- A Dog with Two Tales (*prequel*)
- Dogcatcher in the Rye
- Dark Side of the Moo
- A Streak of Bad Cluck
- Till the Cat Lady Sings
- Alpaca Lies
- Twas the Bite Before Christmas
- Swine and Punishment
- The Cat and the Riddle
- Don't Rock the Goat
- Swan with the Wind
- How to Get a Neigh with Murder
- Tweet Revenge
- For Love Or Bunny
- Between a Squawk and a Hard Place

- Double Dog Dare
- Deerly Departed
- Think Outside the FoxMouse of Ill Repute
- Bee All and End All
- Sheep with One Eye Open
- Roo the Day
- Till Death Zoo Us Part

Bought-the-Farm Mysteries - Boxed Sets

- Bought the Farm Mysteries - Books 1-3
- Bought the Farm Mysteries - Books 4-6
- Bought the Farm Mysteries - Books 7-9
- Bought the Farm Mysteries - Books 1-10

Mystic Mutt Mysteries Paranormal Cozy

- I Want You to Haunt Me
- You Can't Always Get What You Haunt
- Any Way You Haunt It
- I Only Haunt to be with You
- All I Haunt Is You
- Do You Haunt to Know a Secret?
- All I Haunt for Christmas

Books by Ellen Riggs and Sandy Rideout

Dog Town Series

- Ready or Not in Dog Town (The Beginning)
- Bitter and Sweet in Dog Town (Labor Day)
- A Match Made in Dog Town (Thanksgiving)

- Lost and Found in Dog Town (Christmas)
- Calm and Bright in Dog Town (Christmas)
- Tried and True in Dog Town (New Year's)
- Yours and Mine in Dog Town (Valentine's Day)
- Nine Lives in Dog Town (Easter)
- Great and Small in Dog Town (Memorial Day)
- Bold and Blue in Dog Town (Independence Day)
- Better or Worse in Dog Town (Labor Day)

Dog Town Boxed Sets

- Mischief in Dog Town - Books 1-3
- Mischief in Dog Town - Books 4-7
- Mischief in Dog Town - Books 8-10
- Mischief in Dog Town - The Complete Series